D0960937

With Nothing But Our Courage

The Loyalist Diary of Mary MacDonald

BY KARLEEN BRADFORD

Scholastic Canada Ltd.

Albany County,
Royal Province of New York,
1783

October 6th, 1783

They burned the schoolhouse down! A group of Patriots came just as Father was making ready for the new school year.

"Traitor!" they called him. "Cowardly Tory!" All because he would not sign their Oath of Allegiance to the new United States of America.

They seized Father and dragged him out of the school. In front of his very eyes they tossed torches in through the door and the windows. In seconds all was ablaze, Father said. They didn't even allow him to salvage any of his books! What were they thinking? This was their schoolhouse as well as ours. This war has turned everyone insane. Lizzie Crane turned her back on me this morning and would not even give me the time of day. I couldn't believe it. My own best friend. I've been friends with her since we were born!

I cannot bear looking at Father. He is the kindest, gentlest man in the world. He always had a smile on his face and a laugh in his heart. Now he sits at the kitchen table and stares out the window. He will not even talk. Mother is distraught and that makes baby Margaret fussy. Grannie bustles around with her mouth set in that grim line I know so well. I'm not the cause of it now, though, and at least that's a mercy. When Grannie gets mad at you, you'd better skedaddle out of there.

Jamie's the only one who's acting normal. I suppose at five years old none of this means anything to him. He only misses Angus and keeps asking after him. When I told him Angus was off to fight with the British army he thought that a great lark, and went about for days with a stick over his shoulder, pretending to be a soldier.

I don't know what to do. There is no one to talk to. No one to tell me what is going to happen. In desperation I've picked up my old journal. Father gave it to me for my twelfth birthday and I've not written in it yet. Nothing to say, I thought, except news of the war, and I didn't want to even think about that. But I have to now, don't I?

And I'm so frightened! The whole world has gone mad!

October 7th, 1783

I do not know how to write of this. It is so awful I cannot bear it, but I am so full of grief and anger and just plain disbelief that if I do not let it out I will die! How to begin?

They came for Father this morning. A loud,

rowdy bunch of so-called Patriots with cockades in their hats, all puffed up with righteousness and their own importance. We knew most of them. They were our neighbours. People we used to call friends. Lizzie Crane's father was one of them. And Ned Bolton — his wife and Mother have known each other all their lives! They pulled Father out of the house and dragged him down the path. They just dragged him! And then . . .

This is the part I cannot write. But I must.

They lifted my dear father up and sat him on a mule — backwards! They tied his hands to the pommel and whipped the mule forward. They paraded Father through town that way, shouting vile oaths that I cannot repeat even to this journal. My father! He will die of the shame of this.

Then they brought him back and threw him down in the dust.

"Here's a pass for you, Tory," they shouted, tossing a piece of paper after him. He bent to pick it up, but stumbled and almost fell. Mother rushed forward to support him and snatched up the paper.

"Get out of here!" she screamed at the men. Her face was all twisted up and she was crying. "Get out!"

Then she put her arms around Father and he just kind of slumped against her. I started to run toward them but the sound of Ned Bolton's voice stopped me as surely as if he had reached out and struck me.

"Use that pass and be out of here by morning!" he cried. "All of you. We don't want filthy Tories in this town!" Although the word they used was not "filthy." Grannie turned crimson red and

October 8th, 1783

By the light from the campfire

My hands are shaking so that I can hardly write and I've made so many blots I can hardly read what I have written. I feel like a feather bed that's been shaken out, turned upside down and jumped on.

I stopped writing yesterday because just as I was going to say "and put her hands over Jamie's ears," I smelled burning. It was our field! They set our cornfield on fire! And that wasn't the worst of it.

When they finally left, Father turned to us. I have never seen his face look like it did at that moment.

"That is it, then," he said. "There is nothing for it but to leave." It seemed as if he had to force the words out through his lips — as if his mouth wouldn't work. I could barely make out what he was saying.

Mother just stood there. She looked as if she had been struck.

We packed the wagon all night with everything that we could fit into it. And the smell of the burned out cornfield was in our noses the whole time.

We packed Grannie's spinning wheel, Mother and Father's bed and feather tick, Mother's quilting frame, a small chest of drawers, as many pots and kettles and dishes as we could, and a few other bits of furniture. Mother and Grannie packed bags and bags of food and provisions. Luckily we had a good supply of salt pork on hand as Father had butchered our hog last month. I expect we will be eating a lot of that.

We each made a bundle of our clothes. I helped Jamie with his, but we still had to leave much behind. Father tied a cage, with as many of our chickens as could fit into it, to the back of the wagon, but we had to leave the geese.

Grannie insisted on digging up a piece of the lilac bush that grows in our doorway. Granda planted that bush for her when they were married and she said she would not leave without at least a bit of it. It is a very small piece and she has it in a little pot, wrapped in burlap and soaking wet. I do not see how it can survive, but Grannie can be very stubborn when she wants.

We were just getting ready to leave, after a quick breakfast, when those same men turned up again. They'd been into the whiskey, I could tell, never mind that it was first thing in the morning. They smelled of it and they were all red-faced and shouting. Maybe they needed it to get their courage up for what they did.

What they did was rush into our house and push and shove us out. Out of our own home! Even Grannie! They actually knocked her down and not one of them stopped to help her up. I did that. Father had already harnessed old Blue to the wagon and we fled to it. Father climbed up and helped Mother and Grannie up beside him. I gave Grannie a good boost from behind and normally she would have had my scalp for that, but not that morning. Mother was holding Margaret, who began to wail. Jamie and I clambered up in the back and perched ourselves on top of all the things we had packed in there. We'd tied Bess onto the back and she was bellowing because we hadn't milked her. Even the chickens in their cage were making a racket.

And then . . . I don't want to remember, but the pictures are all in my mind and I don't think I'll ever be able to forget them. Even as we watched, those men ran into the house and began smashing things.

Smashing! Smashing! Smashing!

They smashed everything we had left behind — we could hear them doing it. And we could see them through the doorway. They even threw a bench through our glass window.

Why would they *do* that?

The chickens we'd left in the yard were all scattered and clucking and running around every which way in a frenzy. Then I saw a man running off with one of our geese under his arm and I recognized Jed Turner.

My stomach heaved up and I thought I would be sick right then and there. Jed Turner used to be just as friendly as a next-door neighbour could be. Father turned as white as a haunt and without a word he cracked the whip down on Blue's back. Poor old Blue, I don't think he's ever felt such a lash in his whole life. He gave a huge leap and the next thing I knew we were out the gate and down the road, Blue trotting faster than he's ever trotted before and Jamie and me rattling around on top of the wagon like two broken teacups on their saucers. Thank goodness the feather tick was on top or we would have been jounced right off. Bess lolluped along behind us and bawled every step of the way with indignation.

I stared and stared at our house and garden, trying to fix every single detail in my mind until we turned the bend in the road, and then it was gone.

I saw Lizzie looking out her window as we passed her house. She didn't wave. I didn't wave either. We just sort of stared at each other.

We've left our home behind us. Left everything I've ever known in my life. We're escaping to British Canada, Father says. To the Province of Québec. Father told me that Loyalist families have been promised free land there in recompense for their loyalty to the King, but I can't imagine he ever thought we'd be the ones leaving our homes.

I have no idea at all where Québec is, only that it's a long way away from Albany. I am so mixed up and confused and just plain desperate and my head aches *so* badly. I would give anything for one of Grannie's hot teas right now and I wouldn't even complain about how bitter it was, but I don't dare ask her. Things are bad enough. Mother barely had time to cook porridge tonight over the fire that Father built, before it began to rain. We are in the woods with hardly any shelter. Now we are all huddled under tarpaulins and trying to keep dry.

The rain has stopped but the trees are still dripping down on us and everything is so wet it's hard to write without blotching and smearing the words all over the pages. I want to write, though. I need to write.

Mother is feeding baby Margaret, but I can see from here that she is shaking so much that it's making the baby fretful. She has hardly spoken to me at all since we fled and just keeps repeating over and over, "I cannot believe it. I just cannot believe it."

I know exactly how she feels.

Jamie is snoring beside me. He was frightened at first, but now he thinks this is all just a great adventure. It is not any kind of adventure that I would ever have wished. Try as I might, I cannot make sense of all this. For over seven years — more than half my life — this war has been raging. Father has tried to explain it to me. Some colonists wanted independence from Britain. Those are the rebels, or Patriots as they call themselves. Some, such as us, wanted to remain British. For that we are called names and thrown out of our homes! Even Lizzie hissed the word "traitor" at me, but we are *not* traitors. We are *Loyalists!*

Father admits that much of what the rebels claimed was just — the British *were* interfering too much in our affairs, and levying unreasonable taxes upon us. But he never thought rebellion was the answer. He believed so surely that matters could have been worked out, if only there had been enough good will on both sides.

Even though Mother agreed with Father, it practically tore her apart when Angus went off to war. She tried her best to dissuade him, but off he would go.

"Besides," he'd said, "if I don't fight for the British I'll have to fight for the rebels, and that I will never do."

It was after that that our friends and neighbours began to shun us, but we never imagined things would come to this.

I can write no more tonight, but I will tomorrow. It is important, this writing down of things.

October 9th, 1783

Grannie saw how bad I was feeling today. My head was hurting so much I felt dizzy. She made Father pause long enough at midday to brew me up one of her simples.

"Here, lass, this will take the pain away," she said and gave my forehead a rub.

The tea did taste horrid but it made my head feel much better. So did the rub.

Grannie is the only one of us born in Scotland, and she came here as a babe in her mother's arms, but she still has a burr to her voice. It is very comforting — except when she is scolding me. It's hard to believe she is Father's mother; she is so tiny and wiry and Father is so tall. I suppose I get my size from Grannie — or lack of size, I should probably say. And Grannie's so quick and neat about things, while Father is slow and careful. They are really quite different. Grannie can be awfully quick with the switch too but she's always there to make you feel better when you're sick. I guess that makes up for it. Tonight she saw how blistered my feet were from walking and rubbed them with goose grease. They still hurt, though, and I'm bruised all over from being jounced around so in the wagon when I couldn't walk any more.

There are so many trees around here where we're camped that the dark comes early. And it is *so* dark! I have only a tarpaulin spread out over branches above me and I feel like I'm right out in the middle of the woods with no protection around me at all. I've never slept outside at night. I miss the safety of our snug little house. Our campfire gives such a small circle of light, I imagine all kinds of wild beasts just lurking at the edge of it, staring at us. I can hear all sorts of noises and scurrying sounds, too. I even thought I saw eyes gleaming out of the blackness. Grannie just snorted when I cried out, and I suppose it is just my imagination. But maybe it is not. In any case, I have a small tallow wick burning beside me in my shelter at the moment. It will not last the night, though.

Perhaps writing in this journal will take my mind off the dangers out there, real or imagined. I am tired, after our long journeying, but it comforts me to write. It is the only familiar thing I have to hang on to. Thank Providence Father had a whole big bottle of ink at home that he had not yet got around to taking to the school, so I will be well supplied with that for quite some time. I tuck it carefully into a corner of the wagon each morning, well protected by my bundle of clothes.

Jamie just sat up to ask me what I was doing. I had to tell him a story to settle him back down. I think he realized for the first time today that we've really left our home and we might never see it again. Mother won't hear of anyone saying that. "Of course we'll return," she says. "You'll see. When things settle down. We'll be back."

But back to what? We don't have a home any more.

We've been on the move for two days now, heading north, and I am bone weary and sick to death. It is lucky we have that pass, though. We have been stopped twice by rebel patrols and forced to show it. That is very frightening. They point their muskets right at us and act as if they think we are criminals or spies! Without that paper to show that we are travelling by order of our local Committee of Safety, Father says, we would have been in a lot of trouble.

It is so hard, travelling all day every day. Thank goodness the weather remains fine and cool. Jamie and I walk most of the time so that old Blue doesn't have such a heavy load to pull, but we do get tired. Even Mother and Grannie get out when we come to hills. The wagon is heavy-laden and Blue is not used to such continuous work. The road is very rough — not much more than a track in some places. I wonder that Father knows where to go. I dare not ask him as he just sits on the wagon seat, silent, his face as set and stony as a rock. He and Mother hardly talk at all. It is all so different from what it used to be. Father and Mother used to sing and laugh together all the time. Grannie has always been grumpy, but now she really glowers. I don't dare speak to her, either.

All this strangeness is definitely upsetting baby Margaret. At three months old she was just beginning to be a real little person, smiling at every face that bent down to her. Now she grizzles and cries most of the time. I think Mother is having trouble feeding her. Jamie's excitement at this "great adventure" has worn off and he is getting more and more fretful as well. He whines from morning until night until sometimes it is all I can do not to slap him.

We do not seem like the same family at all.

October 10th, 1783

Father sat me down last night and finally had a talk with me. If you could call it that. I didn't have much of a chance to say anything. It's hard to remember that Father and I used to talk *every* night after our evening supper. We talked about what had happened during the day, what I had learned at school, our farm — anything and everything that came to mind. Not all girls went to school, but Father insisted that I should and I was glad of it. I loved school. And I used to love those talks with him, but this one was very different.

He told me that we're going away up north to a place called Sorel, in Québec, on the St. Lawrence River. That's where the families of soldiers in Sir John Johnson's King's Royal Regiment of New York — Angus's regiment — are supposed to meet up. The Royal Yorkers, they call them. There Father hopes we will meet up with Angus, but he doesn't seem to know what we will do after that. Even if we are given land, he has no idea where it would be, or what it would be like. Mother is so certain that we will return home, but if we settle there, would we?

It is all very frightening and confusing.

I tried to help Mother with baby Margaret today but it was no use. Margaret just won't stop crying. I walked her and walked her, and patted her on the back the way Mother does, but nothing helped. Finally Mother reached out to take her back.

"Thank you for trying, Mary," she said to me, "but you'd better give her back. I'll see if I can get her to feed."

But she couldn't. Then Jamie sassed Grannie and she switched him and now *he's* gone all grumpy.

Everything is just as horrible as it can be.

October 11th, 1783

We are stopped now for our noon meal. I am going to take this opportunity to write more.

We have reached the Hudson River and Father says we will follow its valley north from here on. It is a very wide river — bigger than any stream I have ever seen, and the water just seems to rush along in all sorts of ripples and swirls and currents. We are following a track through the trees that runs along the river's edge. Walking is a little easier as there are not so many hills, but watching the river flow back to the land we've left, while we are trudging along in the opposite direction, fills me with sadness. How quickly we are leaving behind all we've ever known and loved!

Mother is calling me. Our meal is ready. It will not be much of a meal, I'm afraid. We have finished up all the bread we brought with us, and Father didn't want to take the time to light a fire so we are just going to have stale johnnycake. At least we have Bess for milk and butter. Grannie puts cream in the churn in the morning and by evening the jolting of the wagon has turned it into butter. That used to be my daily chore. I suppose I should be grateful that I do not have to do it any more. I'm not, though. I would be very happy to be home churning butter right now and I wouldn't complain a bit. Not even to myself.

I am very hungry.

Later

We're camped for the night now. Father shot two partridges and they are roasting on a spit over the fire. That will be a welcome change from salt pork. We can't kill any of the chickens, of course. We will need them for breeding. They have stopped laying, though, and are acting very nervous. One gave Jamie a terrible peck when he was putting their feed into the cage and now he won't go near them again. Mother is boiling up a pot of turnips and potatoes to go with the partridges, but she is not behaving like my dear mother at all. At first, when we stopped here for the night, she just sat in the wagon holding Margaret and staring back the way we had come and didn't make a move to get out.

"Get yourself down from there, Fiona, lass. There's supper to be made," Grannie chided her. Grannie, of course, was bustling around in her usual way and already setting to, getting things ready for the evening meal.

I think Grannie is getting provoked at Mother. Grannie has no patience with what she calls "foolishness." I'm not usually too quick to be helpful, but I was tonight. It is my job to collect wood for the fire and I got to it right smartly. I know what it's like to have Grannie mad at you, and I don't think Mother needs that on top of everything else that has happened.

It's strange — Mother has always taken care of me but now I almost feel as if I must take care of her. She is so distraught and her eyes look so empty.

Later still

The meal was delicious. It is a wonder how a good meal and a full stomach can make a body feel so much better. I'm curled up by the fire now. The night is clear and the stars are so bright the darkness here below doesn't seem quite so dangerous. Sometimes, if I stare up at the stars hard enough, it seems almost as if the world has turned topsy turvy and I am about to fall *down* into them.

The weather was sunny today and any other time I would have enjoyed it enormously. It would have been like when we used to go on outings to visit neighbours or to picnic by the river.

Jamie and I have made a sort of nest in the wagon, padded with the feather bed. We manage to avoid most of the sharp corners and edges of the furniture piled in there and it is quite comfortable. Grannie's little bit of lilac bush waves its leaves above us. Grannie waters it every day and it drips down on us, but I don't mind. Mother passed Margaret back to us, to give her a rest, she said, and the baby slept between us for most of the afternoon. I do love cuddling her when she's not screaming or stinking.

What spoiled the day for me was being stopped by yet another rebel patrol and then passing by two burned-out farms. We hurry through settlements and towns as quickly as possible. There is no telling who would be friendly to us and who would not. As we made our way along the road today, we realized that we were passing through country that had been fought over. The devastation was dreadful! There was nothing left of the houses but blackened stone chimneys, and the fields around them were trampled and all torn up. Even the sheds and the barns were destroyed. Bits of wood and litter were strewn all over the place. It looked like the worst storm in the world had hit here. It made me realize how lucky we were that there were no battles too near where we lived, although one day I did hear gunfire and cannons booming. That was terrifying enough.

Jamie has just come over to nudge me and get my attention. There is a dog sitting at the edge of our campsite, staring at us. He's quite big and has long grey fur, but it's all matted and dirty. I wonder if he is from one of the homesteads we passed by today? I might just sneak a piece of johnnycake to him after everyone has gone to bed. He doesn't look vicious — just sad.

October 12th, 1783

The dog is a hero! I did sneak a tiny bit of johnnycake to him last night. I snuck out of the shelter I'm sharing with Jamie after everyone had gone to sleep. No one saw me at all, not even Jamie, who was snoring away. Mother and Father were sleeping under a tarpaulin with baby Margaret, and Grannie was tucked away in a kind of tent that Father sets up for her. He cuts balsam fir boughs for her every night to spread under her tarpaulin and make her more comfortable because, as she says, her "bones are old and sharp." We just make do with blankets spread over tarpaulins laid right on the ground. Not too bad if it doesn't rain, and the weather is not too cold yet.

But back to the dog.

He was frightened and wouldn't let me near him, so I just tossed the johnnycake to him. He was on it in a split second and wolfed it down. He must have been starving. Then I went back and crawled in beside Jamie, thinking that maybe I could give the dog something else in the morning.

I had just fallen asleep when suddenly the dog started barking and howling and making enough racket to "raise the dead," as Grannie says. Mother and Father burst out from under their tarpaulin and Jamie and I jumped up so fast we knocked our tarpaulin cover right off. Even Grannie poked her head out of her tent. What did we see in the light of the dying fire but three men untying Bess and old Blue! They were going to steal them! The dog was barking at them and charging at them and nipping at their heels. The men seemed quite terrified of him, although one of them landed a good kick on the poor animal's side. Anyway, as soon as we all erupted out of our shelters they took off. You should have heard the cursing and the yelling.

But we still have Bess and Blue. And it seems we might have a dog, too.

It is Sunday today. How strange not to be going to church. I wonder if they will miss us at the service? I wonder if they will talk about what happened? How can they call themselves Christians and do such a thing to us? Our preacher, Mr. Howard, would never condone it, I'm sure of that. But he couldn't do anything to stop it, could he?

Grannie did not want to travel today because it is the Lord's Day, but Father said we had to keep going. She has not spoken to him since.

October 13th, 1783

Jamie is besotted with the dog. He wouldn't ride in the wagon at all today, but walked almost the whole way. The dog followed along, although he still won't come near us. Jamie has named him Laddie and keeps calling and calling him, but the dog doesn't trust us enough to get within kicking range.

Walking was more pleasant today. I am toughening up, I think, and do not get so tired. My blisters have almost all healed, thanks to Grannie's goose grease. The weather is fine and that seemed to lift my spirits a little. Perhaps if I could get Mother to walk a bit more she might feel better, too. I would be glad to carry baby Margaret for her. Mother hardly talks, and looks so sad and troubled that it just tears at my heart. I know it worries Father, as he goes about with his eyebrows all squinched up and his mouth turned down. Not like his old cheerful self at all. Grannie is the only one who doesn't seem to have changed a whit. She is still Grannie. This may sound strange, but that's actually a comfort, even if she does scold me ten times a day for things I really can't help. She used to say I was far too boisterous for her liking and I should have been born a boy. I certainly haven't been very boisterous lately, but I do seem to get in her way a lot.

Still, at least there's one person in this family who is the same as before.

Father says that for now we are heading for a place called Chimney Point. It's on a big lake north of here called Lake Champlain. He figures that at the pace we're going we should be there in not much more than another week. Then, if we're lucky, we will be able to get a boat and continue our way up to Québec. We'll make much better time sailing on the lake than walking around it, he says. But how will they get our wagon and Bess and Blue on a boat, I wonder?

Canada must certainly be a long way away. I wonder what it's like?

October 14th, 1783

It does seem to make me feel better to write in this journal. I can say anything I want here and not be chided. Whenever I complain out loud about anything, Grannie is quick to jump on me. "Things could be worse," she says. "You could be dead."

That doesn't cheer me up one bit.

Mother is beginning to talk more, but now she is worrying about Angus. We haven't had a word from him in months, but we know he was right in the thick of it all. I won't let myself believe that anything could have happened to him. I've already lost one brother — William died of the fever just last year. If he hadn't, he would have been off to war too, even though he was only fifteen years old. William's death nearly broke Mother's heart. She couldn't bear to lose Angus as well, I'm sure, and neither could I, although when he was home he used to tease me to death and was always at me for being so clumsy. I used to get so angry at him. He taught me to whistle though. I'm rather proud of that, although it drives Grannie wild. "Whistling girls and cackling hens," she says, "always come to some bad ends."

Who would ever have thought I would miss Angus so?

The path we're on dwindles down to almost nothing in places and it is very hard to make it out. It does not always follow close to the river and sometimes we have to stop while Father forces his way through the underbrush to make certain that we haven't veered too far away from it. We are thankful, though, that there has not been more rain, as otherwise we would be in ruts and mud right up to the wagon's axles, and the streams we have to cross now and then would be flooding. The leaves are beginning to change colour. The trees are all red and yellow and orange and just glorious. The air is so fresh and crisp I can taste it. Oh, how I used to love this time of year!

My goodness! An Indian has just walked into our campsite! The dog is barking up a storm.

October 15th, 1783

What a scare! When that Indian appeared last night, I leaped up, totally without care for my journal, and it nearly fell into the fire. It's all ashy now and smudged. I was about to run, but didn't know where to. For all I knew we were surrounded!

I've seen Indians around our village in Albany, of course, and am quite used to that, but seeing this one just suddenly standing there in the firelight scared the wits out of me. Mother must have been just as surprised because she leapt to her feet as well. Grannie had already gone to her tent and so had Jamie. Father knew what to do, however. He just stood up and held out his hand to the Indian as calmly as if he had been our parson back home.

"Good evening," Father said.

"Good evening," the Indian replied. Then he said a few words in his own language that sounded like a question.

Father answered him right away in the same language — he had learned a little of it back in Albany from the Indians who traded there, I know. He spoke slowly and haltingly, but the Indian seemed to understand him. Before I knew what was happening, the Indian had settled himself down by the fire and Father had offered him some leftover tea. It was barely warm, I'm sure, but the Indian didn't seem to mind.

I must admit I just stood there staring, frozen, until Mother grabbed me by the hand and pulled me back to my shelter. By this time Jamie had figured out what was going on and he was kneeling under the tarpaulin and looking out, his eyes as big as I've ever seen them.

"Go to sleep, both of you," Mother ordered. Her voice was angry. She sounded as if she had been frightened worse than I. Too much is going on for her to bear, I think.

Before I could say a thing she wheeled about and disappeared into her own shelter.

Neither Jamie nor I had any intention of obeying her, of course. We knelt side by side, watching Father and the Indian. They talked for a long time, in English and in the Indian's own language. I could not understand the half of it, but the Indian's voice sounded very bitter and angry. Finally, he stood up and left. Only when Father had gone to join Mother did I remember this poor journal. I dashed out and picked it up, then ran right back to Jamie. I was certain a hundred Indians were watching my every move.

This morning I felt quite ashamed of myself when Father explained it all. The Indian, whose

English name is John, is one of a party of Mohawks who are also travelling to Canada, and he has good cause to be angry and bitter. It seems that he and his people have been driven from their lands, too, because they fought on the British side, just the way Angus and the other Loyalists did. Their village, which was big enough to be a regular town, was burned, and their homes destroyed during the war. The British had promised to restore their lands to them after the war's end, but instead they gave them to the Americans. Now, in desperation, John and his family are going to join their chief, Joseph Brant, at a place called Fort Niagara. Father told me he has heard a lot about this Chief Brant. His Indian name is Thayendanegea. (Father told me how to spell it.) He is a great leader, Father says.

Anyway, John has asked if he and his band could travel with us for a while. They have had trouble with the rebel patrols and hope that if they are journeying with us things might go a little easier for them. Father was delighted to have them do so. He admits now that he has been very worried as to whether we were on the right track or not, and John knows this country. John says we are all right so far, but that the way gets more difficult, farther ahead. Jamie, of course, can hardly speak for excitement.

Later

I must just add this one bit, although I am now snuggled down under my blanket and can barely see to write.

When I made my way here to bed, I stumbled over something. There was just enough firelight left to allow me to see the dog, Laddie, curled up beside Jamie. He's been letting us feed him by hand today, and I guess he's finally decided we're friends. He looked up at me but didn't growl, so I just crawled into my bed as quickly as I could and tried not to lie too close to him. Jamie is asleep with a big smile on his face. The dog has just let out an enormous groan of what sounds like relief and satisfaction.

He certainly does smell, though.

October 16th, 1783

We've been travelling through deep woods today and Father says he's relieved beyond words that John and the other Indians are with us. They followed behind us and we didn't see them, but John walked with us. When we stopped for the day he and Father went fishing together and Father brought us back three lovely big shad for dinner. John showed us how to clean them, then cook them by burying them in the ashes of our fire until the flesh separated off the bones. They were delicious. I was much more enthusiastic about saying grace tonight!

I find that I'm not getting tired at all now. In fact, it's very peaceful to walk along the track and listen to the birds singing and twittering in the trees high above us. There are just as many squirrels around here as there were back home. Father managed to shoot two of them today for the evening pot. Early this morning Jamie and I went down to the small stream that we were camped beside and Laddie surprised a raccoon washing something in the water. He started to chase after it, but Jamie whistled him off. The dog has adopted Jamie as completely as Jamie has adopted him, and the ungrateful animal has totally forgotten that it was I who first fed him.

Oh, I saw a skunk, too. Thank goodness Laddie did not see it. That dog smells ripe enough without skunk smell added to it.

There are other animals about that are not so harmless. Wolves and bears. And wildcats. The thought of them unnerves me, I have to admit. I lie awake at night sometimes and hear the rustlings and noises in the bush around me and I cannot help but be afraid, even though Father keeps the fire going throughout the night. Last night I heard a cry and I couldn't help but imagine what had happened to some poor small creature.

It's getting colder at night. I wrap myself up in the cosy woolen shawl that Grannie knitted for me, and when Jamie and I go to bed at night I almost appreciate the warmth of that smelly dog. The Indians are camped out of sight, but near us. I can see the smoke from their fire rising above the trees close by, and that makes me feel safer. John and Father talked together for hours last night after the rest of us went to bed. Tonight John brought his son with him to visit our camp. The boy is just Jamie's age. They took to each other right away and soon were playing some sort of game with sticks and stones. Father and John were watching them and it surprised me to see that they both had the same sort of proud, fatherly smile on their faces.

We've been travelling now for more than a week. It seems much longer.

October 17th, 1783

What an incredible sight today! How to describe it? We were following alongside the river for most of the day, although the land along the river's edge was gradually rising and the river was falling farther and farther below us. I could hear this roaring noise that was getting closer and closer.

"There's a waterfall up ahead of us," Father said. "John told me."

I had never seen a big waterfall before and was quite anxious to reach it. Finally, in the early afternoon, John signalled a halt. We could not see the river from where we were, but the noise of it now was so great that we could hardly hear each other speak. John led us through the trees to the bank. When we broke through, what a sight there was to greet us! We found ourselves standing right on the edge. The river raced by us in a smooth, swift, almost oily sheet, then plunged over the brink to cascade down onto rocks far below. Spray billowed up into the sunlight, dancing with rainbows. I have never seen anything more beautiful in my life, but the power of it was fearful. It took me a moment or two to remember to breathe again.

But now we have a problem, Father says. This is where we must part company with John and his band. The Hudson River turns sharply west here, but we must keep on going north until we reach another river that runs into Lake Champlain. John says the name of that river is the Mettawee. Or something like that. I'm not at all sure of the spelling, but that is what it sounds like.

Father is worried that we might get lost, striking out on our own. The track from here on looks very rough and narrow and not well-travelled. He and John are scouting it out right now.

Father has just returned with very welcome news. John has offered to guide us to the Mettawee. It is very good of him to do so, as his family will have to camp here and wait for him to return before they go on. Fort Niagara, where they are going, is far to the west of here and they have just been travelling with us until the river turned and they could turn with it. It will be a long journey for them, Father says, and they might not reach the Fort until early next year. That means they will have to travel during the winter — I cannot imagine how hard that will be.

We are camped close to the riverside and as I write this my ears are full of the sound of falling water. It is strangely soothing. I think I will sleep well tonight.

October 18th, 1783

We have left the Hudson River now. Thank goodness John is with us or we would have lost our way for certain. We are making our way through heavy woods and the track is rough and narrow. It branches out in different directions in several places. Very confusing!

October 19th, 1783

Sunday again. Father said prayers with us after breakfast, but still refused to stay put for the day. Surely the Lord will forgive him, but I don't think Grannie will.

The leaves on the trees are just blazing now — even when the sun is hidden it looks like the forest around us is all lit up. It must be so beautiful around our house. But I won't let myself think of that. It makes me too sad.

I carried baby Margaret for a good part of the way today, even though she is getting heavy. She seems happier when she is carried and does not cry as much. Mother feeds her, then she sleeps, then I carry her for a while. She gurgles and burbles and is beginning to look all around her. A bird flew down and perched on a branch near where we had stopped for our midday break and Margaret squealed at it with great delight.

It seemed to ease Mother a bit, but she is still so unhappy. She does not sing to Margaret. I remember when Jamie was a baby Mother sang to him all the time. In fact, she was always singing, and we loved to sing with her. Her favourite songs were lullabies and old Scottish tunes in a dialect that I never understood the half of. Father loved to sing too, but he favours more rollicking songs and sea chanties. Sometimes when he got quite carried away Grannie would scowl at him and purse up her lips and nod toward Jamie and me and he would have a sudden coughing fit and stop. I suppose those were songs that she didn't approve of. Father may be a grown man, but Grannie still treats him like a little boy every now and then.

Angus's and my favourite song was "The Golden Vanity" and Mother sniffed at it because it was an English sea chanty. "I declare, Robert," she used to say, "I don't know where you pick these things up."

But he never paid her any mind and just kept on singing whatever he wanted to.

I suppose it is a sad song, about a young cabin boy who is betrayed by his captain and left to drown, but we used to sing out the chorus as loudly as we could with all the will in the world, Father's voice bellowing out over all of ours, and we never once thought about what the words were saying. Now I think about it a great deal:

He sank into the Lowland, Lowland, Low
He sank into the Lowland Sea.

We'll be on a boat when we reach Lake Champlain, if Father can get one. I've never been on a boat.

I can't swim. I hope I don't drown!

October 20th, 1783

We have reached the Mettawee. So far we've just had small streams to deal with that were easy to ford, but this river is very wide and the current is fast. It looks dangerous.

John said he thought he could find a better place to make the crossing, so he and Father have gone off to scout for one. Jamie is busy throwing stones into the water for Laddie to chase after and I've had to pull him out twice. Mother is taking this opportunity to feed Margaret. Grannie is looking worried.

Later

We made the crossing, but I'm still shaking with fear. And very wet. Most everything we own is drenched. Fortunately, I was able to keep this journal dry.

Father and John came back and led us farther downstream where they said we could cross. It was not quite as wide as the place where we had stopped earlier, but it was still wide enough to be frightening. I could not help but wonder how deep it was. I soon found out.

And here we had to part with John. He stood watching us as we urged old Blue into the river. I looked back once, then when the current took hold of us I could not do anything but hang on for dear life. When we reached the middle of the river old Blue was almost swimming. He tripped once and the whole wagon tilted. Water streamed in and Mother screamed. I held on to Jamie with one hand and the side of the wagon with the other. I didn't scream, but I must admit I had my eyes squinched tight shut. I just couldn't look. Jamie, of course, worried only about Laddie, who was swimming alongside us.

Suddenly I heard Jamie cry out and I opened my eyes to see the dog being swept down the river away from us. It was all I could do to hold Jamie down. I declare he would have leapt right in after Laddie if I hadn't. As it was he howled and raised a terrible commotion until we finally made it to the other side and onto dry land. Then he was out of the wagon and running down the riverside in a trice.

"Go after him!" Mother cried, but I already was.

Thanks be to goodness the dog managed to make it to the shore by itself not too much farther down. Of course the first thing it did was to shake all over me. As if I weren't wet enough already.

When I thought to look back across the river, John was gone.

Now Father is building a fire and Mother is hanging clothes and blankets up on bushes to dry out. I'm minding Margaret, who has the hiccups. She looks so puzzled every time she hiccups that I can't help but laugh at her.

I am *so* relieved to be across that river!

Grannie has not stopped scolding Jamie since we set up camp. He and the dog make a very woe-begone, wet pair. Bess is bawling. She did have to swim and is obviously not happy about it.

It feels lonely without John. I had not realized how much his presence reassured me. Father says he doubts that we would ever have made it this far without his help, and that he is immensely grateful. Father *must* have been grateful — as well as a goodly amount of our supplies, he gave John the last of his precious tobacco. No more pipe in the evening for him. I can't imagine Father without his evening pipe.

October 21st, 1783

We are to follow this new river now up to Lake Champlain. We should reach the southern tip of the lake tomorrow, and John told Father that

Chimney Point was just another day or two's journey up the eastern shore of the lake. I must admit that I still have a hollow kind of feeling inside of me when I think of what might lie ahead of us.

"I wish John had stayed with us a little longer," I said to Father this morning, but he just smiled and gave me a hug.

"You worry too much, little Mary," he said. "We'll do just fine."

I leaned into his arms and let myself sink into the strength and the warm good smell of him. For a moment it felt just like old times. How I have missed him. Not that he isn't here, of course, but it seems almost as if he is only here in his body. His mind is all closed off. With worry, I suppose. He tells *me* not to worry. How can I tell *him* not to?

October 22nd, 1783

Father was right. We have reached Lake Champlain and the land is beginning to get much hillier. The lake itself does not look so big from here, but Father says he has heard that it gets much wider farther north.

The dunking in the river went a long way to cleaning Laddie off, and Jamie has soaked him in the lake and combed and brushed him within an inch of his life. The dog actually looks quite respectable and has a fine coat indeed. He is as friendly as can be now, and even licked my hand today when I shared a bit of salt pork with him.

He still smells, though. Grannie grumbles about the smell and about giving him our good food, but I caught her giving him a pat, too, when she didn't know I was looking. Her lilac bush is still alive. Woebetide Jamie or me if we sit on it in the wagon!

October 23rd, 1783

I cannot believe how high the hills are here! They are mountains! The track we are following goes along the lake's edge, but it curves and doubles around and at times seems to go straight up and we all have to get off the wagon and walk while Mother drives old Blue. Then the track plunges right back down again and Father leaps back into the wagon and stands on the brakes. We have to stop to rest very often. None of us is able to talk. We have to save all our breath for the climbing.

October 24th, 1783

Chimney Point

We have made it to Chimney Point! Thank goodness the land has flattened out here. The mountains now loom off to the east of us a good distance away. There were times the last two days when I did not think I could walk another step. We are all too exhausted to move.

The lake looks to me to be very wide here, but Father says this is still only the narrow part. There are waves lapping on the shore. I can see some boats out on the water and they look very small and are tossing around in a most alarming way. How big will the waves be when we get out on the wide part of the lake, I wonder? I suppose I should be excited about going on a boat — Jamie certainly is — but I'm not.

The leaves on the hill on the other side are still brilliant, but it is getting quite cold. Father has gone off to see about arranging for a boat. While we wait I will describe what it is like here.

First of all, there are so many people it takes my breath away. Families and wagons and animals are camped all along the lakeside. Some people have tents, some just make shelters out of tarpaulins as we do. There are more Indians around than I've ever seen before. Children are running wild and it is noisy beyond belief. I'm sitting at the edge of our campfire as I write this, on a small rise overlooking the shore. There is a sandy beach below me and Jamie is in his glory. He has made friends with several other children already and they are all barefoot and wet and covered with sand. I would like to walk along that beach, too, but I must mind Margaret, who is sleeping with her thumb stuck firmly in her mouth. Mother is milking Bess. Grannie is napping in her shelter. Now Jamie is trying to get Laddie to fetch a stick. Laddie doesn't seem to see the reason for it and is not cooperating very well and the other children are laughing at him. Jamie has given up and run to retrieve the stick himself.

It would be so nice to be five years old and not worried all the time.

Everyone wants to sail up to Canada, it seems. Except for the people who live here. They are very dour and keep to themselves. Father says they are all Patriots and have no love for us. I can well believe it. One old lady passed me by just now and muttered "Tory cowards" under her breath, but not so much under her breath that I could not hear. I'm certain she meant me to. The scowl she gave me could have curdled milk.

There are still some burned-out foundations of houses around with only chimneys standing.

That's what gave this place its name: Chimney Point. Father gave me one of his history lessons. He told me that this part of the country was originally settled by the French and then, during the war the British had with the French over who would own this country, the British invaded here and all the settlers were forced to flee. They burned their houses as they went and all that was left were the chimneys, standing up tall and lone.

I'm very glad we didn't burn our house when we left. That would have been too sad.

A girl who looks to be just about my age has come up to where we are camped and is standing staring at me. She has the most beautiful long curly hair. She's lovely and tall, too, not short like me. That girl looks nice, though. I think I will go talk to her. It's been so long since I've talked with anyone else my age!

Later

What joy! Her name is Hannah and she and her family are going to Canada, too. You'd never know she's had as hard a time as I have — she just fairly bubbles over with talk. She said when she saw me she was as delighted to see someone else her own age as I was to see her. She said she had to make me take notice of her because her mother had threatened to muzzle her if she didn't be quiet.

"But I can't be quiet," she said. "I just can't. The words all burble up inside me and have to be let out *somehow!*"

Before I realized it, I was talking and laughing with her as if I didn't have a care in the world.

Her family's name is Ross and they lived down in the Mohawk Valley. They've travelled even farther than we have. They have a very fine wagon, though, and the most beautiful brace of oxen I have ever seen. Hannah took me over to their campsite to show the oxen to me and introduce me to her family. Mr. Ross is very fat and bluff and hearty and has hair as curly as Hannah's. He has a really *really* loud voice. Mrs. Ross looks tiny beside him, but she is so bossy with him that I had to hide my face so they wouldn't see me laughing. There is an older sister named Molly and two younger brothers named George and Hugh. The oxen are called Buck and Bright. They are big, but very gentle. Mr. Ross let me pet them. They have the loveliest brown eyes.

Molly seems to take after her mother. She was ordering her brothers and Hannah all around and I wouldn't have been surprised if she had started in on me.

Oh, how I hope we can travel up to Canada together. They are such a nice family and it is so wonderful to have a friend.

Later still

How can I be so pleased one moment and so despairing the next? I had just finished writing those words when I saw Father returning and his face looked like a thunder cloud. I knew at once that something was dreadfully wrong. At first I thought he had been unable to find us a boat, but it was not that. It was worse. He did find a boat, but it is too small to take our wagon! We can only take what we can carry ourselves. We cannot take old Blue, nor Bess — not even the chickens! Mother is beside herself. Jamie is howling and hanging on to Laddie for dear life. He will not be parted from that dog. I am in a daze. How will we survive without our possessions? Without our animals?

My wish that Hannah's family could travel with us has come true, but it is awful as well. They cannot take their wagon or their beautiful oxen either. Mrs. Ross is particularly distressed, Hannah says. She is a weaver and will not be able to take her loom. Hannah told me that it takes a particular skill to make a weaver's loom, and this one was made especially for her mother by a master carpenter back home.

October 25th, 1783

This has to be one of the saddest days we've had since we had to flee from our home. We have spent most of a day unpacking the wagon and figuring out how much we can carry ourselves. It is not much. Mother has wrapped her good china platter in the feather tick. She says she will not move without it. Father has made a bundle of tools. I will carry Margaret, so will not be able to manage much else, but will take what I can. Poor little Jamie will be loaded down with as much as he can bear. Grannie says we must take as many pots as possible but we won't be able to carry many, and certainly not the iron skillets. How will we ever cook our food? She went more quiet than I've ever seen her when she realized she couldn't take her spinning wheel. Her mother had brought it all the way from Scotland with her when she came to America. Grannie will not leave her bit of lilac bush, though. I expect I'll have to carry that, too, somehow. Luckily it is not very big.

Everything is in a heap. Now father is hitching old Blue up to the wagon and leading it away. The wagon is loaded up with all the things we cannot take. The chickens are squawking as if they know something terrible is going to happen to them, and Bess is bawling. I cannot stand it!

At least Father is allowing Jamie to keep Laddie.

"Surely there will be space on that boat for one small dog," he said.

Mind you, Laddie is not small, but the look on my father's face would warn anyone that he has taken as much as he is going to and will not be trifled with further. I've never seen him so angry. He and Mother even had words. I've never heard them argue so before.

"Why can we not just keep our wagon and make our way north by the road?" Mother pleaded when he broke the news to her.

"There *is* no road," Father growled back. It didn't sound like him at all. "Just a miserable track, crossed with rivers that would be difficult for us to ford by ourselves. Besides," he added, "it's too late in the year. It would take us weeks to reach Sorel, maybe months, and we would not be able to make it before the winter snows set in."

"But we can't just leave everything here!" Mother cried.

"I'll sell it all for the best price I can get. The fare for the boat is so exorbitant, we will need the extra money to meet it," Father answered. And before she could get in another word he said, "There's no discussing it further, Fiona," and he turned his back on her! I've never before in my life seen him do that.

Mother is furious and sad and desperate all at the same time. Even Grannie is keeping out of her way.

I couldn't bear to watch Father leading old Blue and Bess away. They've been a part of my life for almost as long as I can remember. To think that they are going to be sold to a stranger! Oh, what if he doesn't treat them well?

Later

Father came back late tonight. He looked sick. I saw Mother look at him and he just shook his head.

"They hate us here," he muttered, so low that I could hardly hear him. "They gave me as low a price as they could get away with."

"Even for Blue and Bess?" she asked. It was not much more than a whisper.

Father didn't answer. He just nodded.

Hannah came by after our supper. She looked stricken, not at all like the smiling girl I met yesterday. Her father has sold their wagon and oxen too, and most of their possessions. The person who bought their loom paid little more than a pittance for it. Hannah said when the man who bought Buck and Bright drove them off she is sure she saw tears in her father's eyes. That is hard to imagine — Mr. Ross was so jovial and friendly yesterday. Hannah says her father said that the man who bought the oxen gloated over the fact that he had given Mr. Ross the lowest price possible.

When she told me this, Hannah began to cry. I reached out to her and then I started to cry too. I couldn't help myself. I haven't cried hardly at all up to now, but suddenly it was all more than I could bear and I just hung onto Hannah and she hung onto me and we cried and cried and cried.

October 26th, 1783

There is a minister here and he held church services this morning. Grannie is much mollified but it hasn't made us feel any better. Still, he prayed for the safety of those of us about to embark on our "perilous journey." I was glad of that. I think we will need all the prayers we can get.

October 27th, 1783

We leave today. We have bundled everything up and are waiting for Father to fetch us. Mother is pacing back and forth with baby Margaret, but Grannie is just sitting like a stone. Jamie is running wild, but she has not said one word to him.

October 29th, 1783

Somewhere along the shore of Lake Champlain

I have not been able to write in my journal for two days because I have been so sick. Everyone is sick except for Father. He almost seems to be enjoying the sail in spite of everything.

I was right to worry about the waves. The lake is huge and the waves are enormous and the boat we are sailing in is so very small! It is a kind of boat called a *bateau,* pointed at both ends with rows of seats for us to sit on. There is no roof or shelter of any kind, so we are praying that it does not rain. We are four families in the boat and we are very squished, sitting three or four to a seat. There is no room to get up or move around at all.

There are five sailors manning the boat: four to row and one to steer, but the sailors are happy because the wind is so strong that they can run with the sail up and do not have to row. We stop on the shore each night, but only long enough to make a fire and eat — that is where we are as I write this — and then it is back into the boat again. It is very uncomfortable sleeping all squashed up, but the sailors prefer to keep going at night as long as there is a good wind. I do not know when they sleep.

Even though the sailors make up a good stew for us each night, or else fry up fish that they have caught in the lake, I have not been able to force the slightest morsel down. Even the smell of it makes me ill. Perhaps I will die.

Hannah is as sick as I am; so are all her family. At this rate her father will be much less fat by the time we reach Canada. He already looks different. He is sick, as we all are, but it's more than that. He looks smaller, somehow. As if the air had been let out of him. Even his voice has shrunk.

One of the other families in the boat is the Denny family. They are going to settle in a big town in Québec called Montréal. They are very grand and are travelling with their own slaves! (Who they make sit at the very back of the boat.) Of course they don't call them slaves any more, just servants. Father says that that's hypocrisy, though. They're just as much slaves as they ever were. The only Negroes that are really free are the escaped American slaves who fought with the British armies, Father says.

The Dennys have three little children, but Mrs. Denny won't let them talk with us. The Negro family is composed of the parents, Obediah and

Lisa, and a little girl named Tam. Tam is a quiet little mouse of a thing, but very sweet. She is peeping at me from behind Lisa's skirts right now as I am writing this.

They are calling for us to get back on the boat. I am going to be sick again.

October 30th, 1783

The strangest thing. I awoke this morning and felt as well as if I had never been ill at all. The boat was skimming along and the wind just seemed to be blowing right through me. I felt fresh and new and alive again. And hungry! We just had johnnycake and cheese that Father had purchased at Chimney Point, but it tasted wonderful. Mrs. Ross dug into a bundle she had at her feet and pulled out a jar of blackberry jam.

'The last of my preserves," she said. "I left dozens of jars in our wagon. I suppose someone else is enjoying them now," she added, then she shrugged. "Oh, well, I'm sure there'll be blackberries aplenty in Canada."

She does seem to be able to "put a good face on things," as Grannie says, although it is obvious that she is making an effort. Hannah tells me she will not speak of the loss of her loom. I wish Mother could be as brave. Mrs. Ross tries to be friendly, but Mother just sits and broods. She definitely does not like the boat.

Now that we are both feeling better, Hannah and I are beginning to enjoy the sailing. Hannah is back to her usual self and talking ceaselessly. Her mother puts her hands over her ears in desperation, but I enjoy Hannah's talk. It is so good to have a friend again!

It is a lovely feeling to be sailing over the water so freely, and the waves are not quite so frightening. I just hang on tightly and let the water spray over my face. It is refreshing. In fact, Hannah and I were actually leaning over the edge to catch even more spray until Grannie put a stop to it. We were both drenched.

"You look like drowned rats," Grannie said with a sniff.

I suppose she does not think Hannah is any more ladylike than I am. And she's not. And I'm very glad of it.

October 31st, 1783

The wind died down today and the sailors were not happy because they had to row, but I quite liked it. The waves calmed considerably and the boat moved along in a much more relaxing manner. The lake stretched ahead for as far as I could see and the mountains rose up high on both sides of us, right down to the shore on the western side. I just sat back and drank in the sight.

We are camped now on a long, wide beach. Hannah and I tore off our boots as soon as we got out of the boat and just raced along it. The cool sand felt glorious between my toes. It was just a short respite before we were both called back to help with chores and minding babies, but it was enough. Best of all, we do not have to get back on the boat tonight! Now that they must row, the sailors prefer to spend the night on land. They have distributed tarpaulins for shelter and we have made ourselves quite comfortable. It will be lovely to sleep on land again, with a blazing fire going outside our shelter.

We had fresh fish that the sailors caught for supper, rolled in flour and fried in lard in a skillet over the fire. To go with it we had johnnycake and boiled turnips. I am sitting by the campfire well bundled up in a blanket and I feel very full and satisfied. Laddie is happy too. He was more ill than any of us but was delighted to get a piece of my well-toasted fish skin. At the moment he is running around in circles like a mad thing, chasing his tail. Grannie is trying to look disapproving, but not very successfully. I think she is as pleased as we are to be camped here so comfortably. She has been just miserable on the boat. Not that she complains, but I can tell.

Now I can write more of what has been happening these past days. There is so much to say!

George and Hugh were a veritable nuisance on the boat today. It was much quieter when they were sick.

"A right pair of imps they are," Grannie says. I think she's right, as I pulled George away from the railing of the boat several times and no sooner had we come ashore than I found Hugh trying to braid Laddie's tail. It's fortunate indeed that Laddie is such a good-natured dog.

I don't know what Hannah's mother would do without Molly, as her bossiness comes in very handy for controlling those two little boys. They are a handful.

Hannah has an Uncle Allan who is also with Sir John Johnson's Royal Yorkers, which is why her family is going to Sorel too. They hope to meet up with him there, as we are hoping to meet up with Angus. I wonder if her uncle knows Angus?

Now Mother is calling me to go to bed. Father has just walked by and put his hand on my shoulder. He saw that I was writing in my journal and gave me a smile. That pleases him.

It is nice to see him smile again.

I gave Mother an especially big hug before

crawling into my shelter and she gave me a squeeze back.

"You've been such a help, Mary," she said to me. Then Margaret started grizzling and she went to soothe her, but I didn't mind.

Goodnight, Journal. There is a small little spot in my heart that feels *almost* warm again. *Almost* happy.

November 1st, 1783

Still on Lake Champlain

A good southerly breeze has sprung up again and we're fairly flying along. Father was sitting beside me today and he was humming under his breath. Our song. The one about the sea. So I joined in, very softly at first, but gradually we both got louder and louder until we were sitting there with the wind blowing all around us and the smell of the water in our noses and singing at the tops of our voices.

He sank into the Lowland, Lowland, Low,
He sank into the Lowland Sea.

Hannah was sitting on the other side of me and I taught her the words. She's a grand singer and soon the three of us were just roaring the song out. Father had his arm around me, and Hannah and I had our arms around each other. Mrs. Denny was shocked, I think, but Mrs. Ross, who was sitting with Mother, just smiled. Then George and Hugh started playing war with Jamie and Jamie — who is younger and smaller than they are — fell off his seat trying to get away from them, and Laddie started jumping all over George and Hugh, trying to protect Jamie, and the helmsman yelled at them all to sit still and not rock the boat, and soon all three were crying.

Quite a commotion in a very small boat.

November 3rd, 1783

Canada!

We have reached the top of Lake Champlain and are in Québec. It doesn't look one bit different from America, but the land is not as mountainous as it was at the southern end of the lake. I can see forests stretching out on both sides of us, but no hills to speak of.

We are not getting off our boat yet, though. We are going to continue up a river that flows out of Lake Champlain, the Richelieu River, as far as we can to a place called Fort St. Jean. Every name is French because this all used to be New France before the British won it.

Hannah and I have become fast friends. She is

by far the nicest person I have ever known. And the prettiest. But she doesn't even seem to know or care how pretty she is. Not like Lizzie Crane who was always on about how fair her skin was, and how she didn't freckle the way I do.

I do hope we will be able to stay together.

I'm beginning to worry again. These days on the boat have almost seemed like a piece out of time. Nothing seemed really real. But now we're back to real with a thump. I wonder what we will find when we reach Sorel?

November 4th, 1783

Fort St. Jean

A near disaster today! Tam fell overboard! This is how it happened:

Our boat was drawing up to the docking place at Fort St. Jean and Tam got so excited she leaned too far over the railing. Her poor mother was busy trying to round up Mrs. Denny's three little treasures and could not keep an eye on her. I was the only one to see her go over as everyone else was busy getting ready to get off the boat. I happened to be watching her and was just about to reach out and pull her back when splash — over she went! I didn't even stop to think, but jumped right in after her. It was only when I landed in the water that I remembered that I couldn't swim! Thank goodness it was shallow and I found my footing immediately. Tam was not so fortunate, however. She is quite small and the water was over her head. She was thrashing and sputtering about like a hooked fish and I had a dreadful time getting hold of her. Finally I did, and managed to hand her back up to her father.

Lisa and Obediah came over to where I am sitting now by our fire, in dry clothes with a blanket wrapped around me, drinking catnip tea that Grannie brewed for me. Lisa was almost crying and she just kept saying, "Thank you, oh thank you so much for saving my baby," over and over. Obediah shook my hand most formally.

Grannie, however, has not stopped upbraiding me since it happened. I suppose she doesn't consider that kind of behaviour proper for a young girl. But what was I supposed to do — let Tam drown?

The weather is very cold and I truly thought I would never stop shivering, but the tea is warming me up and I finally have.

I feel sorry for Obediah and Lisa, having to work for such an unpleasant family. Mr. Denny is a dour, unfriendly man. In all this time he has barely spoken to Father or to Mr. Ross. Considers himself much above them, I suppose, because he is wealthy and managed to come away with most of his wealth intact. (I heard Father say that to Mother one evening. I'm not quite certain what "intact" means, but I imagine it means he's still got his money. He wears a fat money belt around his waist. Maybe that's where it all is.)

It must be horrible to be their slaves. Poor little Tam. It must be horrible to be anybody's slave! They are all leaving us here, though. They have made arrangements to hire a wagon and will go west to Montréal. We will set out with the Rosses for Sorel. On foot. With no wagon. Our wealth is not intact.

It is going to be difficult.

November 5th, 1783

Québec

We are following alongside the Richelieu River. The going is very hard even though there are few hills, thank goodness. We are all loaded down like pack horses. Grannie has insisted on carrying her lilac bush, even though I offered, and it is looking very bedraggled. Most of its leaves have fallen off and I'm afraid it might be dead. There's no saying that to Grannie, though.

Hannah and I walk together, but we are both so encumbered that we can hardly speak. Baby Margaret was very sick the whole time on the boat and does not seem to be getting over it. She vomited all over me and even though I tried to wash it off in the river when we finally stopped, I can still smell it. Father has rigged up a kind of sling for me to carry her in and that helps, but now it stinks, too. I was very glad to hand her back to Mother to be fed this evening.

Salt pork and turnips for supper.

I am too tired to write more.

November 10th, 1783

I am almost too weary at night to write in this journal, but I will make myself add a bit to it before I sleep. We walk all day with only a brief stop for a cold meal. It has been raining for the past two days and by the time we stop for the night we are all soaking wet and shivering with the cold. We attempt to dry our clothes out by the fire, but they are still damp in the morning. I try to keep baby Margaret as dry as I can, but she cries constantly. She doesn't seem to be feeding very well and Mother is fretting. I wish we had Bess — then we could make Margaret some sops with johnnycake and cow's milk. She is too little to eat anything else.

Hannah is such a good friend. She carries her

own load and tries to lighten mine when I am carrying the baby. There are times when I truly feel I cannot put one foot in front of the other and I am so grateful for her help. *She* would never act the way Lizzie Crane did.

November 12th, 1783

The rain has stopped but we are still damp and dripping. I saw something very unusual this morning. Almost frightening. When I went down through the trees to the river's edge to wash, the morning mist was just beginning to clear. I looked up across the river to the other side and there, looming out of the fog, I saw a hill — a mountain, really, but such a mountain as I have never seen before. It sat in the middle of a flat plain, all alone, with a cloud covering its top and mist swirling down its sides. The slopes were covered with trees, scarred here and there with steep, bare rocks. There were no other mountains or hills around at all, just that one. It looked so mysterious — so gloomy and ominous. I felt a shiver go right through me.

For some reason I could not speak of it to anyone, not even Hannah. I hope it was not a bad omen.

November 13th, 1783

Father encourages us on. He assures us that we are nearly at Sorel. We have passed quite a few settlements and the people are much more friendly. They mostly speak French, so we cannot talk to them, but they are kind. A woman gave us a whole pan of milk and some fresh bread today. I fairly gulped down my share of the milk, and my portion of bread was gone in three huge bites. It tasted so good! She even tossed a bone to Laddie, who nearly wagged his tail off in gratitude. Father taught Jamie and me the French word for thank you.

"Merci," we said, and the woman fairly beamed back at us.

Grannie was able to make a nice mush for Margaret but she was so fussy she wouldn't eat it. I see Mother trying to feed her now, but Margaret is just crying and crying. Mother looks quite frantic — I wish there were something I could do. Mrs. Ross is helping as much as she can, but nothing will make that baby stop wailing.

Thank goodness it is no longer raining, but the weather is much colder. I think I can smell snow in the air. Father always used to tease me when I said that, but I was right so often that sometimes he would even ask me if I thought snow was coming. I certainly hope I am wrong this time, though. How could we possibly make our way through snow?

November 14th, 1783

Sorel, on the St. Lawrence River

We arrived at Sorel late this afternoon. It is a military encampment on the south shore of the St. Lawrence River. This river is most certainly the biggest I have ever seen. It looks calm and flat today, but I can sense a powerful current flowing underneath the surface.

"Surging all the way to the sea," Father said as he stood beside me, staring at it.

There are so many people here at Sorel that compared to this place, Chimney Point was quiet and peaceful! First, there are all the barracks for the soldiers, then there are tents for all of us *refugees*. That is how they refer to us, *refugees*. The soldiers have been very good to us. They gave us a tent to stay in and some blankets and food. They even gave Father a little tobacco, so he will be able to have his pipe after dinner again.

The Rosses are camped right next to us and we shared our supper tonight. We built a huge fire and feasted to our hearts' content on boiled fish, turnips and potatoes, and we are all warm and dry. Baby Margaret has a tummy full of warm milk and is finally content. I played with her and she is now trying to catch at anything that comes within reach. She has developed a funny little laugh that sounds just like a tiny rooster crowing. Hannah says she thinks she looks like me. Poor baby!

As soon as the arrangements can be made we will cross and sail a little farther down the river to another camp which has been made for the families of the soldiers and officers. It is called Machiche, and we will winter there.

"And after that?" I asked Father, but he just shrugged.

"We don't know yet, little Mary," he said.

"After that we'll be going back home, of course," Mother snapped. "Things will surely have settled down by then."

Father just looked at her and didn't answer.

I don't think we'll be going back home.

I'm not sure I want to. There's no way I will ever forget what happened.

November 15th, 1783

Father went off early this morning to talk to the officer in charge . . . Oh — I see him coming back now. There are two soldiers walking alongside him. I wonder why he's bringing soldiers with him. They are dressed in such ragged uniforms, they look like scarecrows. One of them walks just like

Later

I am so excited I can hardly write. It was Angus! It is almost two years since I have seen him! Even though he's only five years older than I he seems so much older and so different now, I'm almost afraid of him. Isn't that strange?

Mother is so happy! When she saw Angus I thought she would fall down in a dead faint. She got all white and gaspy and clutched her apron so hard she tore it. Then she just ran at him and hugged him until it's a wonder his ribs didn't crack. She hasn't stopped smiling since. I can't remember the last time I saw her smile.

I felt quite shy when he came up to me and tousled my hair the way he always used to. I used to hate that and get really cross when he did it, but I didn't today. I was just so glad to see him that I loved it.

"Hello, Mouse," he said, just the way he always did. He always used to say that I looked just like a little brown mouse and I hated that, too, but today it made me feel warm and happy. I could almost believe he'd never left except for the fact that he is so thin and he looks so much older and so very tired.

Angus was in an enemy prison camp and he escaped. But that's such a story I shall wait and write of it tomorrow. We sat and talked by the fire so long that it's far too late to start in on it now.

Oh, yes. The soldier who was with him. His name is Duncan. Duncan Morrison. He was imprisoned with Angus and it was his mother who got them out. Oh, what a tale that is! I will have such fun writing it down!

Duncan is very quiet. He hardly spoke a word — just let Angus do all the talking. He is as thin as Angus and looks just as worn out, but there is something else about him. His eyes look very sad.

He looks . . . haunted. That is the only word for it.

The Rosses all came over to make Angus's acquaintance. Hannah, of course, never stopped asking questions the whole time they were here. She thinks Angus very well-favoured. That surprised me. Angus is just Angus — my brother — I've never thought of what he *looks* like. I suppose he is "well-favoured" though — I saw Hannah's older sister Molly looking at him out of the corner of her eyes. He was looking back, too. For a moment I thought he was going to speak to her, but then George fell into the fire and created a stir. He wasn't burned, but his clothes got very dirty and black and Mrs. Ross was angry with Molly for not watching him better. No wonder Molly is often cross and bossy. Those two boys are little devils. The Rosses left soon after that but we stayed on talking for ages.

Father and Angus are still talking, in fact, but I must go to sleep. My eyes will not stay open. Mother has gone to settle Margaret, and Jamie and Grannie are asleep too.

November 16th, 1783

We had proper church services today and it did raise our spirits. There was much to be thankful for. And there was more good news as well. Hannah's Uncle Allan is here! Mr. Ross met up with him this morning and now the Ross family is celebrating. The only sad thing is that when we leave for Machiche tomorrow, Angus and Duncan will not be able to go with us. They must go to rejoin their regiment at a place farther upriver called Fort Cataraqui. Hannah's uncle is to go to Machiche with us, though, and join the soldiers stationed there. Mother was very upset when she heard that Angus would not be coming with us.

"It's just for the winter, Mother," Angus told her. "We are to help build grist mills and sawmills to be ready for all the settlers next spring. Sir John Johnson has purchased land from the Mississauga Indians all along the river, and that is where Governor Haldimand of Québec is planning to settle you. When you arrive at the place chosen for you, I'll join you there."

Mother's face darkened. "We will be going home next spring," she said. "We will not be *settling* here."

"Fiona," Father began. He stopped. He and Angus just looked at each other and didn't say a word. I suspect this is what they were talking about last night after we had all gone to bed.

Mother didn't say another word, but tightened up her mouth in that stubborn way that looks just like Grannie's when she's set on something, grabbed baby Margaret from out of my arms and went back into the tent.

There is going to be one mighty problem here. But I am not going to worry about it now. Now I am going to write the story of how Angus and Duncan escaped.

Angus and Duncan were both in the 2nd Battalion of the Royal Yorkers and they were captured together by a rebel patrol when they were out on a scouting foray. They were sent to a terrible prison near Albany and found themselves sharing a tiny, dark hole of a cell there. It was filthy, Angus said. They were given hardly any food, and precious little water. A lot of the other prisoners were getting sick and they were afraid they'd become sick too. Angus said that at night they just lay on rags on the floor and he could feel the rats scampering over him. I would have gone mad!

"I wouldn't have lain down," I told Angus when I heard that. "I would have stood up all night!"

"We were there for months, Mouse," he answered, with a peculiar twist to his mouth. "Sooner or later you have to lie down. After a while you don't even notice the rats crawling over you — you're just grateful if they don't bite you."

"Oh, Angus!" Mother cried when she heard that.

I can't imagine what it would have been like.

Anyway, it seems that Duncan's farm was not too far away and one day who should appear to visit them but Duncan's mother. I don't know how she found out he was there, but she did. She took one look at the pair of them and told them she was going to get them out of there by hook or by crook. (She sounds very much like Grannie, I think.)

This is how she did it. She began bringing in

food and fresh bedding for them and taking the soiled linens home to launder. The guards became quite used to that because many other women were doing the same thing. There were women going in and out every day, in fact.

Then, one day, Mrs. Morrison didn't bring their bedding back. Instead, when she unrolled her bundle, there were two dresses and shawls in there.

"Be quick with you now," she ordered Angus and Duncan, "before the guards see you. Put these dresses on over those uniforms and cover your heads with the shawls. Then just keep your eyes lowered and walk out with me."

"We never believed it would work, but it did!" Angus said.

I looked over at Duncan and was about to ask him a question about his mother, but the look on his face stopped me. I would have thought he would have looked as excited as Angus was at the telling — proud even, of his mother — but no such thing. In fact, he suddenly leapt to his feet and strode a few paces away, then stayed there with his back to us. Angus gave him a concerned look, then continued with the story, but in a more subdued tone of voice.

There is definitely a mystery here.

Anyway, to go on . . .

They watched and chose a time when a whole group of women were leaving together, then they just joined them and walked out with them. The guards didn't even notice.

After Angus and Duncan had escaped, they determined to head north to Canada. They had heard that the families and soldiers of their regiment were gathering at Sorel, so they made their way here as quickly as they could and arrived just two days ago. Angus said he was hoping so much that he would meet up with us here, but could hardly believe that it would happen.

Father reached over to give Angus a hug and Mother started fussing around him again and brought him a cup of tea.

"You have to build your strength up," she said.

Even Grannie was after him, bundling a shawl around his shoulders to keep the night air off him.

I don't think anyone but me noticed Duncan slip off into the shadows.

It must be so hard for him to see all of us so happy when he had to leave his family behind in Albany — but something tells me there is more to it than that.

November 18th, 1783

Machiche

We crossed over the St. Lawrence River today in another *bateau*. Angus did not come over with us, of course, for he will soon be leaving for Fort Cataraqui. He must get there before the river begins to freeze up. Mother was terribly unhappy to have to part with him again, but he reassures us that he will see us in the spring as soon as the river opens up.

There was just enough wind to let the sailors use the sails, but not enough to make big waves. Because we were going downriver we sped along at an unbelievable pace. It was lovely, except that I was wild with impatience to see what was awaiting us on the other side.

The St. Lawrence River is as wide here at Machiche as Lake Champlain at its widest. If it weren't for the current I would think we were on a lake.

Father just walked by and told me that it *is* considered a lake here and is called Lac St. Pierre.

Machiche itself is crammed full of people like us, Loyalists who have escaped from the Colonies. Some of them have been here for months, even years. The soldiers have built a whole town full of little log houses for us all. They are just shanties, really, with hardly any space between them, and the streets are narrow mud tracks that wind all around and between the buildings. There are dogs running loose all over the place. Jamie is keeping Laddie close to him on a bit of string as some of the dogs look quite mean, and growl when you approach them. It is very crowded and dirty. Still, it will be better than sleeping out in the woods. Especially since the weather is getting colder and colder. They have a school, too, and I will be able to go to it.

More good news is that the cabin we have been allotted is very close to the Ross family's.

November 19th, 1783

We have settled in. This cabin is so small! When I think of our lovely house back in Albany . . . But no, I won't think of it. We are making do, that's what is important. There is only one room. Mother and Father have curtained off a section of it with an old blanket — that's where they and baby Margaret will sleep. Grannie has made up her bed beside the hearth. Jamie and I will sleep in a kind of loft. The only way to get into it is by a ladder, through a hole cut in the ceiling. I like it, actually, it is very cosy; but Jamie is cross because he cannot teach Laddie to climb the ladder. I am rather relieved about that.

The privy out back is horrible. We share it with about four other families. Enough said about that.

Mother and Father have the feather tick that we brought with us, but Grannie and Jamie and I make do with blankets that the soldiers have given us, spread over balsam fir boughs. Grannie has her own blanket but Jamie and I have to share. Only one blanket for every two children is the rule. Fortunately, we have the quilts that we managed to bring with us. Father says he will make Grannie a proper bed first thing. Grannie snorted when he said that, and said there were plenty of other things that needed doing before that, and her bones weren't that old, but I imagine she will be grateful for it in any case.

I must go. Baby Margaret is grizzling again. She has caught cold and her poor little nose is so runny she can hardly breathe. She fusses and will not feed or eat the warm sops that Mother makes for her. Mother and Grannie have not said anything, but they have worried looks on their faces when they tend to her.

November 22nd, 1783

Too busy to write much these past few days — and too tired. We have been given a bake kettle, a tea kettle, an iron skillet and an iron pot for cooking. Also a meagre supply of salt pork (I am *so* tired of salt pork!), flour, ground corn and oatmeal. Some of the settlers who arrived earlier on got sugar from Montréal, but there is none of that left. There is maple syrup, however. Also salt. We have a small barrel full. We have also been supplied with a few pieces of furniture: a table and two benches. Grannie is demanding a spinning wheel but Father says that will have to wait until we are settled permanently. He said that out of Mother's hearing, however, as she refuses to hear of us not returning to New York Province in the spring. (New York State, I should say, now that it is a part of the new United States of America.) We have no wool for Grannie to spin in any case.

The salt pork tastes very odd. I think it has gone bad. Father has gone off to hunt.

The neighbours have been very helpful. They brought over johnnycake and bread and oatmeal for porridge. Mrs. Livingstone, whose family lives just a few cabins away, came over this morning with a crock of yeast starter so that we can make our own bread. It's not like the bread we used to bake at home. This is made by mixing salt and sugar into mashed potatoes and water. When you keep the starter in a warm place it gets all bubbly. That's what makes the bread rise. Every time we use a cupful we must top it up with more flour and potato water. Bread made without that is as hard as a rock. I know. We have been eating that since we arrived here.

Margaret continues poorly.

November 23rd, 1783

There is a Presbyterian preacher here, his name is Mr. Murchison. He held services today for us in his house. It was very comforting. But cold. The snow has finally come and the wind is howling.

At first I was disappointed that there were no windows in our little house, but now I am glad. That would make it even colder. My loft is freezing. Mother puts stones on the hearth to heat up and Jamie and I take one each, wrapped in a rag, when we go to bed. By morning they are cold again, though. I almost wish that dog *could* make it up the ladder. At least it would be another warm body up here.

November 24th, 1783

Father shot a deer today! He and Mr. Ross — Uncle Andrew, he has told us to call him, and Mrs. Ross will be Aunt Norah — have cut it all up. We will feast tonight, and the weather is cold enough that we will be able to keep the rest of the animal hanging up outside the door, well out of the reach of Laddie, and any wild animals that might venture near.

November 25th, 1783

Jamie and I are to start school soon. Unfortunately for Father, they already have a schoolmaster here in Machiche. His name is Mr. Mitchell. I think Father is very disappointed.

Baby Margaret has stopped fussing. She just lies limp in Mother's arms. Her breathing is so raspy! Grannie has made a poultice for her chest but it doesn't seem to be helping any. I am frightened for her. I wish there were something I could do.

November 26th, 1783

I almost cannot bear to write this.

Baby Margaret died!

When I came down from the loft this morning I knew at once something dreadful had happened. Mother was sitting at the table with her head down on her arms, weeping. Grannie was holding Margaret, but the baby was all wrapped up with only a small bit of her face showing, and she wasn't making a sound. Grannie was not trying to soothe or rock her. She was just holding her. Then

I heard hammering behind the house. (It was Father, I found out later, making a tiny coffin.)

Jamie burst down the ladder, calling to Laddie. I grabbed him and hauled him outside. I saw Hannah and told her what had happened. Then Uncle Andrew and Aunt Norah came right over. People kept coming by all day long. Even people we have not met yet. Mr. Murchison sat with Mother for a while and prayed with us. Jamie kept hunched up in a corner, all white-faced and quiet. Some of the women tried to comfort him but he just shrugged them away. Any other time Grannie would have had his hide for being so rude, but she just patted his shoulder whenever she passed him by. He is huddled up in bed beside me right now and is making little distressed-sounding snuffling noises in his sleep. First we lost William, now Margaret.

Grannie took charge and made certain everyone was made welcome and thanked for coming, then she made us a cold supper after they had all left. Mother wouldn't eat. She went into her room and I have not seen her since. Father's eyes were all red at supper too.

We will bury Margaret tomorrow in the small Presbyterian graveyard.

The poor wee baby. She was just beginning to be a person. I keep thinking of the way she used to gurgle and smile at me . . .

I have to stop writing. My tears are blotting the paper and making a terrible mess.

December 1st, 1783

I have really been too sad to write in this journal this past week. Mother has been walking around the house like a ghost. Grannie is doing most of the work.

We have started going to the school. I was looking forward to that so much, but all of the fun went out of it when baby Margaret died. I will write of it anyway and see if that makes me feel any better.

Hannah and I went together the first day, of course. The school is in a shanty on the other side of the settlement. It is just one room. We have long tables set up as desks, with benches to sit on. Very few books — only those that Mr. Mitchell brought with him. We have been provided with a few slates and we take turns using them. Mr. Mitchell has set Hannah and me to teaching the youngest ones their letters. There are two other girls the same age as us. Their names are Annie Stanton and Flossie Hoople. They seem nice.

Most of the others are boys. Father had decreed that I should take Jamie, even though he is so young, and George and Hugh went as well. George is a year older than Jamie and Hugh a year older than that. I thought they would be a terrible nuisance, but the teacher, Mr. Mitchell, is very good at keeping order. Perhaps too good. Father was good at keeping order, but he was never mean. I think Mr. Mitchell is mean. He has already strapped two boys for no more than what Father would have considered normal high spirits.

There are about twenty children there in all. Jamie, George and Hugh are the youngest. Several of the others are around my age, only a few are older — all boys. The older girls, such as Molly, seem to feel they should be at home helping their mothers. Or, perhaps it's their mothers and fathers who feel that way. I am very fortunate in having parents who have told me that I can keep on going to school for as long as I want. Hannah says her mother and father have told her the same. Of course, once we leave Machiche, there is no telling when we will find another school.

I told Father about Mr. Mitchell strapping the boys. Father looked disapproving, but only said that sometimes strapping is necessary.

"Boys like to test the Master out," he said. "It is important to let them know right away that disorderly conduct will not be tolerated."

I don't think he really approved, though. It

must be hard for Father seeing someone else doing his work.

One thing is a little difficult to bear. I am used to being the top girl for my age. No one has ever been able to best me at reading, spelling or ciphering, but Hannah is just as good as I am and, I must admit it even though it galls me to do so, she can out-spell me! I was most annoyed when she won the spelling bee today. Still, I like her so much I suppose I can put up with it.

I miss Margaret so terribly. I keep thinking I hear her cry and looking around for her. I remember I did that for so long after William died — I kept expecting him to walk through the door. Sometimes when my mind was wandering I even laid a place for him at the table before I realized what I was doing.

I do not feel any better at all.

December 3rd, 1783

School goes on. I think Alex Calder is sweet on Hannah. He sits and stares at her with such a moony expression. He did not even hear Mr. Mitchell ask him a question this morning.

I teased Hannah about it when we were eating our lunch but she blushed and got quite annoyed with me. I think I had better not tease her again.

I don't suppose any boy will ever be sweet on me.

December 5th, 1783

It is so strange not to be making ready for the winter. Usually by this time we would have had the harvest in and would have been busy putting down potatoes and vegetables in our root cellar, drying apples and salting pork in barrels. We always killed a pig and used "everything but the squeal," as Grannie would say. I used to hate helping Mother boil the fat down for lard and soap, though. It smelled so bad! But I guess that was better than what Angus and William had to do. They had to scrape the bristles off the dead pig so Father could sell them to the general store for a bit of extra money. That was truly disgusting. The whole business was messy but the hams hanging up in the fireplace chimney to smoke made it all worthwhile. I'm not that fond of salt pork — and getting less and less fond of it — but I do love smoked ham. This year we will have to make do with the rations we have received from the soldiers and what Father can shoot.

It is unusual for Father to be home all day at this time of year, too, and he seems very unhappy about it, but he says that hunting and fishing will keep him busy. People fish here even in the winter. Father says they cut holes through the ice!

We have a barrel of salt pork sitting outside the door (what joy!) but no hams. No strings of dried apples hanging over the hearth, either. Potatoes and turnips, but no root cellar to put them in. Father is digging a hole next to the house and that will have to do. He has made a kind of shelter there. Grannie has brought her bedraggled lilac bush into the house for the winter and it sits in a corner, well wrapped up in burlap. It looks very dead to me, but Grannie does not give up easily.

We have so few clothes and no means yet of making more. We will have to make do with what we wear on our backs. We have been promised by Governor Haldimand that we will be supplied with bolts of cloth and blankets from the King's stores, but I fear that those who arrived before us have received most of them. Nor do we have a bootmaker here to make us new boots when the ones we are wearing give out. Some of the settlers have learned from the Indians how to make moccasins — perhaps we will as well. We could make them out of the hide of the deer that Father shot, once he has it tanned.

It is going to be a long, difficult winter. And so lonely without William, Angus and Margaret. We seem like such a small family now. No wonder Mother is so sad.

December 6th, 1783

Mr. Mitchell gave me another bottle of ink yesterday. I was despairing because I was running out, but when I screwed up the courage to ask him for some to take home, and told him what it was for, he gave me a whole bottle! He was very impressed that I am keeping a journal. I thought for one horrible moment that he was going to ask to see it, but thanks be he didn't.

Perhaps he is not as mean as I thought he was.

December 7th, 1783

Hannah was here at the crack of dawn to fetch a shovelful of coals. Somehow or other their fire went out last night. Father is careful of ours. He banks it every night and covers the coals with ashes. Jamie is very proud because Father has given him the job of whittling a stick of wood into shavings every evening, to use to coax the fire back alight in the morning. Father gave him his own knife to work with and it is Jamie's dearest possession. Next to Laddie, of course, who is snoring by the hearth as I write this.

December 8th, 1783

We have had a message from Angus to say that he and Duncan arrived safely at Fort Cataraqui, and are busy with the rest of their battalion helping to build a sawmill. We will probably not hear from them again until spring, but I think that message raised Mother's spirits a little. She is still very despondent, though, and Grannie is twice as bossy to make up for it.

It's strange how I go along for several days feeling almost content, and then I wake up one morning feeling homesick and miserable. I miss baby Margaret and keep remembering all of her sweet little ways. It seems so unfair that her life should have been so short.

How I wish things could be as they were. I wonder if I will ever be happy here?

December 9th, 1783

The cabin of a family named Roberts caught fire today! We had just settled down to our morning lessons at school when we heard a great clanging of a bell and people shouting. Of course we all piled out to see what was going on. A cloud of smoke was billowing up from the north end of the settlement. Hannah and I tore over to see what was happening. As we got close we saw flames leaping up out of the roof of the cabin. There was so much smoke it made us choke. It didn't help, either, that there was a brisk wind blowing. Men were running toward the fire with buckets of water, and women with quilts. They soaked the quilts in water and threw them on the burning roof and on the rooves of the houses next to it. At first it didn't seem to help at all, but gradually they got the fire under control before it spread to the other houses. Then it began to snow and that helped as well. The cabin was saved but it will have to have a new roof. Mrs. Livingstone's quilt was burned clear through. Grannie ran out with one of hers, but by the time she got there the fire was out. I'm very glad, because it was the quilt from my bed. Of course, I would have sacrificed it if it were needed, but I'm mightily relieved that it wasn't. The nights are *cold* here.

Father says the fire was probably caused by sparks from the wooden chimney. That's why he won't burn pine wood in our fireplace. It's too gummy and causes the chimney to soot up. Even so, I could see sparks coming out of the chimney when I went out to our privy to relieve myself before coming to bed. I hope our roof doesn't catch on fire!

I'm tucked up cosily in my quilt now, though, with the stub of a candle to give me light. Mother has told me that I mustn't keep it lit for too long. Candles are much too precious to waste. I suppose I should put it out now.

December 10th, 1783

All the women are getting together to try and find scraps to give to Mrs. Livingstone so that she can make a new quilt. Her daughter, Janet, asked me at school this morning if we could give them some. I asked Mother when I went home at noontime, but she just shook her head.

"Our very clothes are scraps — what could we possibly give them?" she asked.

I felt embarrassed and dreadful all at the same time. I didn't know how I was going to go back and face Janet. Then, just as I was leaving, Mother thrust something into my hand.

"Give Janet this," she said, and ran back into her room before I could answer her. When I looked at what she had given me I saw that it was baby Margaret's old blanket.

I cried all the way to school, but managed to stop before I got there so that no one would see. Hannah saw, of course, because we always walk together, but I didn't mind that. Hannah and I have no secrets from each other.

December 11th, 1783

Janet says she and her mother and her older sister, Betsy, have started piecing together the patchwork for a quilt top already and they are very grateful for all the material. Janet says her mother has promised us all a quilting bee in the spring as soon as they are ready to put it together. I must practise my stitches this winter and maybe I'll be allowed to do some of the quilting. I am quite a neat stitcher, even if Grannie does nag at me all the time.

Actually, it's probably because Grannie *does* nag at me all the time that I have become so good. Perhaps I should not get so cross about it.

I smell snow in the air again.

December 12th, 1783

My nose was right. It snowed all night and is still snowing. My feet froze on the way to school today. I envy the people who have good Indian moccasins to wear.

December 13th, 1783

Still snowing!

December 14th, 1783

Snow has stopped and I would dearly love to go out and play in it but it's Sunday. Church services this morning and church services again this evening. Mr. Murchison preaches very long sermons. In between times we are supposed to sit quietly and not even play. Grannie does not let us do anything on Sunday!

I am writing this up in my bed where she can't see me. I suppose that is very bad of me, but I just have to do something.

I am feeling so twitchy. My legs just want to *run!*

December 15th, 1783

Today we had a snowball fight at school, girls against the boys. It was so much fun. The boys are bigger but I think the girls were cannier. Alex Calder hit Hannah squarely with a huge snowball. I told her that proves he's sweet on her. So she hit me with a snowball and got snow all down the back of my neck. She says that all boys are dolts and she wouldn't want to have anything to do with any of them, much less Alex Calder. I don't think I believe her, but that's one subject I think I had better not pursue. She's quite fierce about it.

That's why I don't believe her.

My one and only dress and my coat were soaking wet when I got home, of course, and Grannie was angry. She says I am a little heathen. How could I be a heathen when I go to church services every Sunday?

Anyway, my clothes are all draped over the bench and table, steaming away in the heat from the fire. The whole cabin smells of hot, wet wool. I am sitting as close to the hearth as I can, in my nightdress and well bundled up in my quilt. I feel quite warm and comfortable, actually.

I must stop writing now and practise my stitching.

I think the girls won the snow fight, but the boys will never admit it.

December 16th, 1783

It is my birthday today. I am thirteen years old. If we were still in Albany I would be celebrating with Lizzie Crane and my other friends from school. There would probably have been presents. No presents here. I don't think Mother has even remembered it. I did not tell anyone at school, but I did tell Hannah. She gave me a hug. That is a good enough present for now.

Later

Father came in with four squirrels and Mother is making a stew for supper.

"For our Mary's special birthday dinner," he announced.

So I guess they didn't forget after all.

The stew is bubbling away and beginning to smell very good.

Later still

The stew was delicious. So much better than mouldy old salt pork. And there *were* presents! After dinner Father presented me with a doll that he had whittled himself. I am much too old for dolls, but I did not tell him that. Jamie gave me an apple that Mrs. Leake had given him last week. He had hidden it away for me all this time, the scamp. He worried that it was a little dried up and shrivelled, but I assured him that it was perfect. I cut it neatly into five pieces after supper and we all shared. I have saved the seeds to plant when we are finally settled somewhere. We had apple trees back in Albany, but I suppose now we will have to start over.

Mother did not have raisins or currants for a cake, but she made Lumpy Dick and we had that with maple syrup. All in all, it was a feast!

And just now, as I was about to climb the ladder up to my bed here in the loft, Grannie stopped me.

"Here, child," she said, and gave me a small square of embroidered linen. It was one of her fine handkerchiefs that she had embroidered herself for her marriage chest. It bore her initials, M.M. for Mairi MacDonald — the same name as mine although mine is written in the English spelling and hers in the Scottish. For once she was smiling and her face looked all soft. Looking at her in the firelight, I suddenly realized that she must have been very pretty when she was young.

It has turned out to be a lovely birthday, after all.

December 19th, 1783

Father says that news has come that the English have now completely evacuated New York City and the last of the Loyalists have left America. General Washington and Governor Clinton made a triumphant entry into the city on horseback. I truly do not believe we will be going back home, no matter how much my mother wishes to. I don't want to, either. Why would we want to live amongst those people again after the way they treated us? I certainly would never be friends with

Lizzie Crane again. Hannah is a much better friend. I do hope that when we settle we will be somewhere not too far away from each other.

December 20th, 1783

Everything is all abustle because Christmas is coming. The Scots don't celebrate the way the others do, but it is exciting nonetheless. Back in Albany the English would bring in a huge log — a yule log, they call it — and they kept it burning for the twelve days of Christmas. The Irish lit candles and placed them in the windows to welcome Mary and Joseph. The German families had the best custom of all, I think. They used to bring in a live fir tree and set it up in a corner, and decorate it with candles! The Rickles had an enormous tree and we children all went over on Christmas Eve to watch them light the candles. It was so beautiful I could hardly breathe. They could not leave them alight for long because of the danger of fire, but it was bonny while it lasted.

Scots go to church on Christmas Day and have our festivities on New Year's Eve when we celebrate Hogmanay; but we'll be celebrating Christmas as well this year because Mrs. Livingstone is going to invite us to her house for a grand Christmas dinner.

Father had a terrible time persuading Grannie to go. She's very set in the old ways and dead against making any kind of celebration out of Christmas itself.

"A papist custom," she snorted when the invitation came. "You'll not find me taking part in it."

Nevertheless he persevered. Father is just as stubborn in his own way as she is in hers.

"It's a new country with new ways, Mother," he said, and would not let up on her, but even so I was amazed that he managed to convince her.

Could Grannie possibly be mellowing?

One thing Grannie will never give up is her determination to go into the New Year without a speck of dust or dirt anywhere. She and Mother are cleaning every corner of the house and it is worth a body's life to get in their way.

December 25th, 1783

What a day! I am sitting here in my bed just full of the smells and tastes and memories of it. There was sadness, too, though.

Mrs. Livingstone gave us the most wonderful Christmas dinner. They have been here for almost three years and are so well settled in they even have a small flock of chickens and a few geese. Mrs. Livingstone had fattened one of the geese up especially and roasted it for the Christmas dinner — I can't begin to describe how delicious it tasted. When Mr. Livingstone opened the door to greet us, the smell of that goose absolutely overwhelmed me. I just stood in the doorway and sniffed until Grannie gave me a push and said, "What ails you, child? Get in before you let all the warmth out."

Mrs. Livingstone had even managed to save raisins to make a plum pudding. It was a feast!

Their house is a little bigger than our cabin but still, it was packed with all of us. The Livingstones have two young boys as well, and a baby. The two boys took Jamie in hand the minute we were inside, and were soon playing a game of knuckle bones with him. The baby was fast asleep in a cradle beside the hearth and never cried once the whole time we were there. She is a sweet, rosy-cheeked little thing. It made my heart ache to look at her, it just brought back so many thoughts of baby Margaret. I can't imagine how Mother must have felt. I didn't even dare to look at her. I think Mrs. Livingstone knew, however, as she gave Mother a very warm hug.

Mrs. Livingstone calls the baby her "first little born Canadian." That made me stop and think. What are *we* now? We're certainly not American any more, and we're not really Scottish any more either. I suppose we're Canadians too. How very odd.

After the dinner Janet and her sister, Betsy, showed me the quilt they were piecing together. I recognized the squares that came from baby Margaret's blanket. It was a pretty, soft yellow colour. I remember Mother dyed it that colour with goldenrod blossoms.

Mrs. Livingstone came over to us just then and reached out a hand to touch one of the squares.

"So soft," she said. "And so pretty. I am grateful to your Mother, Mary, for letting me have that blanket. Small enough return have I made for it."

And I realized then that she knew whose blanket it had been.

December 27th, 1783

Now we are getting ready for our own celebration. Mrs. Livingstone gave Grannie some honey so that Grannie can make the special oatcakes sweetened with honey that she bakes for us every New Year's Eve. We will take as many as we can over to the Livingstones' to reciprocate for the fine Christmas dinner they gave us. It is not much, but it is the best we can do.

Hannah has been over and we have been helping Grannie. At least, we thought we were helping. Grannie thought otherwise, and after she rapped my knuckles sharply with her spoon, just because I dipped a finger into the honey pot, she banished us out of the house.

I can hardly wait for New Year's Eve. There are quite a few Scottish families here, so Hannah and I and the other Scottish children will be going singing at the doors of every house, just as we used to do in Albany.

But I wonder if a first-foot will knock on our door at midnight? Who will it be, here in this strange place?

January 1st, 1784

Get up, gude wife, and dinna sweer,
An' deal yer bread to them that's here,
For the time'll come whan ye'll be dead
And then ye'll need neither ale nor bread.

That's what we sang when we went door to door, and my how we sang! And we reaped such rewards! I had oatcakes and bannock and plum cakes enough to share with the whole family.

The first-foot did come! Just exactly at midnight, by the old clock that Father managed to bring with us, there was a knock on the door. There stood Uncle Allan Ross, holding a loaf of bread and a pail full of burning coals to add to our fire. Warmth and comfort for the whole year to come, the first-foot brings. I wonder if that will hold true for us? Luckily Uncle Allan Ross does not have red hair. Grannie firmly believes that it would bring very bad luck upon a house if the first-foot were a redhead. Father scoffs at her, but she will not be convinced otherwise.

I looked around, suddenly realizing that Father was not here. I supposed he was returning the favour and acting as first-foot for the Ross family. (Hannah told me this morning that he had.)

So we begin a new year in a new land. And I have a dreadful head cold and a very sore throat. And a cough. So does Hannah.

January 3rd, 1784

Grannie has been filling me full of her remedies. She has been dosing me with a syrup made of spikenard, which is as sharp and bitter as its name, and I have drunk enough catnip and spearmint tea to sink a ship. The remedies must be working, though, as I am getting better.

Hannah is not, however, although her mother has the same medicines.

January 5th, 1784

Hannah is very ill. I am frightened for her. When I visited her today she was flushed and feverish and hardly even knew I was there. Her breath is raspy and I can see the effort it costs her to breathe. She can talk hardly at all and coughs without ceasing. I sat with her all afternoon and tried to get her to drink the teas Aunt Norah had made for her, but she could not get them down. Then she spit up the little she did manage to swallow.

January 6th, 1784

Hannah might die! No one has said so, but I can see it in their faces. Father has allowed me to stay home from school so that I may sit with her and feed her.

January 7th, 1784

Our preacher, Mr. Murchison, came over to sit with Hannah and Aunt Norah today. They are certain she is going. I cannot bear to think of it!

January 9th, 1784

Hannah moans and tosses in her bed. She does not recognize me when I speak to her. I put cloths soaked in cool water on her forehead, but she is so feverish and hot that they dry up within minutes. Aunt Norah is beside herself with worry.

January 10th, 1784

Mother does not want me nursing Hannah. I think she worries that I might take the fever next. I will not stop, though.

January 11th, 1784

Mr. Murchison prayed today for Hannah at Sunday services.

January 12th, 1784

Hannah is no better, but neither is she any worse.

January 14th, 1784

The fever seems to be lessening.

January 18th, 1784

We begin to have a little hope. I prayed extra hard for Hannah today.

January 20th, 1784

Hannah awoke this morning pale and weak, but clear-eyed. The fever has gone!

I am happier than I can say, but so exhausted I cannot write more.

January 26th, 1784

I am back to school now, but Hannah is not. She is still weak and Aunt Norah insists on her resting up until she gets her strength back. Truly, it is just as well that she doesn't try to go to school, as the weather has been very cold and stormy — one blizzard after another, it seems. The schoolhouse is drafty, too. Mr Mitchell keeps the fire going full blast in the stove in the middle of the room, but even so my fingers get so icy that I can hardly write, and my feet are wet and freezing cold all the day long.

It is so strange to be there without Hannah. Her empty desk beside mine looks so forlorn. I do hope she will be able to come back soon.

January 30th, 1784

I have just returned from visiting Hannah. She is much recovered, and we spent a cheerful hour just talking. She is propped up in a bed beside the hearth, well tucked in. Molly is even being nice to her and not the slightest bit bossy. The two boys were so rambunctious, though, that Aunt Norah turned them out of doors to find wood for kindling.

Aunt Norah says Hannah is too weak to go back to school before spring, but who knows what we will be doing by spring? It seems that Mother is not the only one who hopes to return home. Others are talking that way as well. Father will hear none of it, however, nor will most of the men. The officers of the Regiment maintain that it would be impossible, and I am very afraid that they are right.

Sir John Johnson is buying up land from the Mississauga Indians for us to settle on, but there is a lot of concern about heading upriver to such wild lands. Governor Haldimand said that the British Government has promised the Loyalists enough supplies and provisions to get us established. We are due no less as a reward for our loyalty and to recompense us for our losses, the Governor said, but Father and the other men want to see proof that he can fulfill his promises, so the Governor has written to England for that assurance.

Mother leaves the room whenever Father talks of these plans.

February 1st, 1784

Another month begun. My life has settled down into such a routine — sometimes I even forget that I haven't lived here forever. Maybe not quite, but I am finding it more and more difficult to remember what home was like.

Home. What a sad word. I don't suppose I shall ever have a home again.

February 3rd, 1784

Hannah is almost back to her old self again, but she is very thin and tires easily. Grannie sends soups and broths over to her with me every time I visit.

The weather is truly horrid. It was sleety and rainy all last night, and this morning the snow was covered with a layer of ice. Jamie and the Ross boys are out sliding down the piled-up mounds. I can hear them shrieking with glee and Laddie is barking his head off.

Oh dear. I hear more shrieking, and it is decidedly not gleeful . . .

Later

I suppose it was to be expected. I ran out to see what was the matter, and there was Jamie, lying on the ground, white and senseless, with Laddie nosing him worriedly. He had tried to slide off the roof of a shed and fell. What a scare!

When Mother saw him lying there she just started to cry and shake and couldn't do a thing. I think she thought she'd lost another child. It was up to Father to pick him up and bring him into the warmth of our cabin. He soon recovered and is sitting beside me here by the fire now, where I can keep an eye on him. Laddie is curled up as close to him as he can get, and the smell of hot wet dog is pretty strong. Jamie has an enormous bump on his head and Grannie has made a vinegar-and-smartweed poultice to put on it. For once he seems chastened.

Father was quite cross with him, which wasn't like Father at all. I think we are all chafing at being so shut in during this horrible weather. Grannie is missing her spinning wheel. Normally we would spend the winter knitting the wool that Grannie spun. I used to complain about always having so much work to do; now I find it hard not to have something to occupy my time. We do have a drop spindle, the one I learned to spin on, but we have no wool to spin even on it.

I think also that Father was out of sorts because he has a toothache. Even Grannie's remedies do not seem to help it.

February 7th, 1784

What a dreadful day! Mother and Father had the most awful argument – and they never argue! It all started at breakfast time when Father said he was going to attend a meeting to do with planning how we will be moved west up the St. Lawrence to our new settlements in the spring. Mother's hands started trembling. I was standing right beside her, waiting to receive a bowl of porridge from her to put on the table, and I could see her fingers suddenly clench the bowl. Just as suddenly, it slipped out of her grasp and fell to the floor. She made no move at all to wipe up the spilled porridge. Instead she just stared at Father.

"Surely, Robert, you are not *really* planning on taking us all upriver into the wilderness?"

"What else can we do?" Father asked her. He was rubbing at his cheek and his face looked tired and drawn with pain. That tooth is bothering him more and more and he has been very out of sorts.

"We can go home, that is what we can do," Mother answered. "Back where we belong."

"Where we *belong?*" Father burst out. I have never seen him so angry. "Why must you insist on believing we still belong back in Albany? Was it not enough, Fiona," he roared, "that I was publicly humiliated? Made to ride backwards on a mule through town for all to see and jeer at? Was that not enough? Do you want to see me tarred and feathered and ridden out of town on a rail — possibly even hanged? We do not *belong* there any more, and that is what will surely happen if we return! I've heard the stories of those who have tried. Besides, what do you think we would have to return to?"

Jamie and I were shocked into silence. Even Grannie was speechless. This was not the Father we knew.

"Our house and lands are gone," he went on. "Do you think they would be given back to us? We have nothing left in that new *United States of America,* Fiona. *Nothing.*"

"But surely, Robert," Mother began, "by now — "

"By now there is someone settled in our house and working our land and glad to be rid of us," Father said.

His voice was not Father's at all. It was so bitter! The words seemed to catch in his throat and he stopped for a moment. Then he gave himself a huge shake and went on.

"Canada is our country now," he said finally, "We belong here. There's opportunity for us and we must make the best of it. We can never go back."

Mother stared at him for one long moment,

then she let out a cry and ran into their room.

I could not stand it. I ran after her. She was stretched out on her bed, sobbing. I knelt beside her and reached out to her, trying to comfort her. She just shook my hand off.

"Go away, Mary," she said, her voice all muffled and shaking. "Just go away."

So I did.

She has not come out of her room all day.

February 9th, 1784

Mother and Father are being very cold to each other. I do not know what to do. I have never before seen them act this way. Grannie is worried too and it is making her very cross.

She has just made a hot fomentation for Father, though, as his tooth is still paining him.

February 10th, 1784

Poor Father. He is lying down in his room now and I just heard a faint moan. In spite of all Grannie's hot fomentations, his tooth just got worse and worse. Finally, he had to have it pulled today and I have never seen a person go through such pain.

One of the men in the settlement here, Joss Walker, has a turnkey and some experience as a tooth puller. He came over late this afternoon. He brought with him a jug of whiskey and set it on the table. Mother looked at it and set her lips.

"Robert does not take whiskey," she said.

Grannie took her arm. "Leave it be, Fiona," she said. "He will need it."

"Mary, Jamie, outside with you then," Mother ordered.

"But Mother," I argued, "there's a fair blizzard blowing out there." Truth to tell, I was afraid to leave. I did not know what was going to happen and I feared for Father.

"Then up to the loft," Mother said. "And be quick about it."

Jamie and I scurried up the ladder, but then lay quiet as mice and watched what went on below.

Father lifted up the jug and took a mighty swig of it. Then he coughed and sputtered and made a terrible face. Nevertheless, he took another drink, and then another. Again that grimace . . . and then yet another swig of the whiskey. He stumbled as he put the jug back down, and Mr. Walker reached out a hand to steady him and help him sit down. No one in the room spoke a word. I was overcome with dread.

"Don't watch, Jamie," I said. He was even more frightened than I, and crept off to huddle on his bed tick.

I saw Father grasp the rungs of the chair so hard his knuckles turned white. Then Mr. Walker took out his pocketknife and began to pry at the tooth with it. I heard Father grunt with pain and my stomach took a lurch. Then Mr. Walker inserted the hook of the turnkey and began to pull. I saw Father's forehead break out in great drops of sweat and he could not help but groan. Mother let out a cry and Grannie put her arms around her.

It seemed to take forever. Mr. Walker pulled and pulled and my poor father hung onto the chair and tried so hard not to howl with pain. Finally there was one last tremendous tug and one last cry from deep down in Father's throat, and Mr. Walker held up the bloody tooth.

Father swayed in the chair and I thought he would faint, but Grannie was quick to hold the cup of whiskey to his lips and he took a long drink. Then Mother helped him up and with his arm around her shoulders she supported him into their room. He has been lying down in there ever since, and Mother has been cooling his cheek with one of Grannie's poultices.

I am still feeling sick to my stomach.

Poor Father!

February 12th, 1784

I am very very tired of being cold. It just keeps on snowing and snowing. My boots are wearing out and by the time I get to school in the morning my feet are wet and frozen. How I wish I could have knitted myself some new mittens. My old ones have holes in them and my fingers get frozen and it's so cold in the schoolroom that they never warm up. Mother has given me a blanket to pin around my shoulders and wear when I have to go outside. I keep it on all morning while I am doing my lessons.

I just counted up. I have not seen the sun for seven days.

February 15th, 1784

The dissatisfaction in the community at the thought of being forced to go upriver this spring to settle in wild and unknown lands is increasing.

"There's no one there but Indians and a few French trappers," Uncle Andrew said when he was visiting last evening. "And all the land is heavily forested. We will have to be assured of plentiful supplies and help."

"Governor Haldimand is promising that very thing," Father answered. "Besides, Andrew, the Regiment will be staying together. We will be with friends and we will have the officers to help us."

Uncle Andrew just puffed on his pipe and did not look convinced.

February 20th, 1784

I am in disgrace. Grannie is glaring at me even as I sit by the fire and write this. I'm trying to get back into her good graces by tending to the evening stew and looking very virtuous and industrious, but I do not think it is working. And all because of that wretch, Danny Snyder. This is what happened.

When I got to school this morning I must admit I was not in a very good mood. I was cold and wet and it is snowing again. Still snowing, I suppose I should say, as it never seems to stop. I'm sure the weather was never this dreadful back home. In any case, when a snowball hit me on the head and splattered freezing wet snow all down the back of my neck, I was furious. I whipped around and there was Danny grinning like a great booby. Without stopping to think, I grabbed up a handful of snow and threw it back at him as hard as I could. How was I supposed to know there was a lump of ice in it? And that Mr. Mitchell had chosen just that moment to come out of the schoolhouse?

Mr. Mitchell never saw Danny throw his snowball, just the one that I threw. It hit Danny square on the nose and the ice made it hard enough that it gave him a good thump and wouldn't you know it, his nose began to bleed.

Well, you've never heard such howling. I should think a big lump of a boy like that would be ashamed. Twice as big as me he is, and he cried like a baby. Terrified he was when he saw that blood streaming out.

Mind you, I was a little concerned myself. For a moment I thought I'd killed him.

Mr. Mitchell practically dragged me into the schoolroom. For a moment I thought he was going to strap *me,* but he didn't — girls never get the strap. He did lecture me soundly, however, and made a point of walking home with me after school to tell the whole family about my "unseemly" behaviour. Grannie is furious, Mother says she is deeply disappointed, and Father shook his head.

I do believe I saw just the ghost of a smile twitch at the corners of Father's mouth when he turned away, though.

February 29th, 1784

As if this month hasn't been bad enough, it would have to have one extra day in it!

March 3rd, 1784

Two days of sunshine! It feels splendid, even though it is still freezing, and the ice on the river is beginning to show soft spots. That brings its own worries, however. Mother has set me to watching Jamie like a hawk. He is not to go anywhere near the water. That is a nuisance, but I am feeling so light and happy that I can put up with it.

Aunt Norah says Hannah might be able to come out for a short time tomorrow.

March 4th, 1784

It seems like those beautiful two days were just sent to taunt us. It is snowing again today and just as cold as ever. Hannah was even more disappointed than I, she had been looking forward to going out so much.

March 10th, 1784

The mood in the settlement has changed completely. Governor Haldimand announced yesterday that he had received word from England promising us all the supplies and assistance we will need. Now, instead of grumbling, people are beginning to make plans and even look forward to our journey upriver. We are to go as soon as the river is open — probably late April or May.

Mother looked stricken when she heard the news. I think she was really still hoping that something would happen to prevent this. It is settled now, though. We are going for certain. I must admit to a queer little feeling of excitement inside me. What will it be like, I wonder?

March 15th, 1784

The sap is running! Mr. Mitchell closed down the school and the whole community turned out to help. I've always loved maple syrup making time. We've been working for days collecting the buckets of sap and lugging them over to the boiling areas where the big iron kettles are hanging over the fires. Everyone does what they can, even Jamie and the other small children. They can barely manage one bucket apiece, and not even that if they're very full. I'm proud to say that I can carry *two*. That dim-witted Danny Snyder made me a wager that I couldn't, but I did. I had to because the penalty was that I would have to give him a kiss if I couldn't. As if I would let that happen! I only agreed to the wager because Annie Stanton and Flossie Hoople looked so horrified when he suggested it. Also, Grannie wasn't anywhere around.

I balanced a yoke over my shoulders and let a bucket hang down from each side of it. It was hard work, especially forging through the snowdrifts, but I'm very sturdy.

We made syrup and sugar as well and there will be enough for all of us. Grannie could not help herself – she turned up to oversee the boiling. She fancies herself the best judge anywhere of when the syrup has reached the right stage. It had been boiling all day and we watched it slowly change from a pale, watery sap to a rich, dark golden colour. Grannie was there with her ladle to test it and when she dipped it in and a long, stretchy thread hung down from the ladle, she pronounced the syrup done.

The best part as far as I'm concerned, of course, is scooping the syrup out of the kettles and throwing it onto the snow to harden into taffy. We all just munched and munched on it – even the adults. I saved the biggest piece I could for Hannah.

March 20th, 1784

Would you believe it? We are having *another* snowstorm! But I don't even care because we are going to have a quilting bee. Mrs. Livingstone and her daughters have finished piecing together the top, and many of the women in the settlement will get together to help quilt it to the batting and the backing. I am practising like mad so that I will be allowed to help, and rubbing my hands with goose grease every night so they won't be too rough and scratchy. Up until now I've only been allowed to thread needles. This time I'm going to quilt!

March 25th, 1784

The weather has turned sunny and all the snow is dripping and melting. I heard a bird singing a lovely spring song this morning. Hannah came out today to sit in front of her cabin and we just soaked up the sunshine. It is still chilly of course, so we kept her well bundled up, but it was such a joy to see her outside. The quilting bee is the week after next, and she will be able to go so we practised our stitches.

I am terribly afraid that she is neater than I and her stitches are tinier. Oh, what if she is allowed to quilt and I am not?

April 6th, 1784

The quilting bee was yesterday. I couldn't write about it last night because it was so late when I finally tumbled into bed. Now I must write everything down so I won't forget it. As if I could! I've been to bees before, of course, but never was one so special. And so welcome after such a long hard winter in this strange new place.

I'm sitting outside in the sunshine and even though my fingers are cold and there is still a chill breeze blowing, I am determined to stay out here. I have found such a delightful spot to write in. It's in back of our cabin where a little grove of cedar trees makes a kind of secret place. I just discovered it yesterday. No one can see me here. It is so peaceful. There is nobody else around — just me and the birds who are singing their hearts out. Mother is watching Jamie and I have a great swatch of time all to myself before I must go and help with the noon meal.

This is what happened at the bee.

When we arrived, Mr. Livingstone had just taken Mrs. Livingstone's quilting frame down from where she hangs it from the roof above her bed. He made it for her and was very proud of it. Mr. Livingstone walks with a limp because he was wounded in the war, that is why they came up here so early on. He could fight no longer and their neighbours were set to hang him for a traitor if he stayed. He just barely escaped with his life, and Mrs. Livingstone had to follow him and bring the children with her all by herself! Janet and Betsy told me all about it while we quilted. And yes! I was allowed to quilt with the women. So was Hannah. But I'm getting ahead of myself. It is so hard to write things down in the proper order. My quill just wants to race ahead and get it all down as fast as possible.

We pushed the table aside and made room for the frame, then set benches all along the sides. The boys were shooed out of the house and Mr. Livingstone disappeared to do some work outside. He is an excellent carpenter and much in demand here. Aunt Norah is hoping that once we are settled he will be able to make a new loom for her. I held my breath while the women took their places and set the younger girls to threading needles. Some of them were charged with taking the smaller children out to play. Hannah and I just stood there. I was feeling very shy and I know she was, too.

"You girls, come and join us," Mrs. Livingstone said then and made room for us. "According to your mothers, you are both accomplished stitchers by now. I'll welcome your help."

Well, I'm certain my face almost split in two I was smiling so hugely, but I sat down beside Hannah without a word and took up a needle.

We worked for the whole day and finished the quilt off by late afternoon. The women chatted the whole time — talk of babies and recipes and such. No one chose to speak of the war. I was seated next to Mother and for the first time since we were forced out of our home, I saw her face relax and soften. She loves to quilt but it has been so long since she has had a chance to do so.

"My fingers will have forgotten how," she said at first, apologizing, but she needn't have. Within minutes her hands were fairly flying over the quilt and I declare her stitches were the tiniest and most regular of them all.

Only when the talk turned to the coming journey did her fingers falter but, surprisingly enough, most of the women were making their plans to move with very few qualms.

"It will be a blessing to be in my own home again," Mrs. Livingstone said. "We hewed our home out of the woods in Albany when we were first wed, and I see no reason why we cannot do so again."

The words were so brave.

"Do you not wish ever to see your own home again?" Mother asked, her voice not much more than a whisper.

"Many a time," Mrs. Livingstone answered. "But it is not to be. Canada is my home now."

Mother fell silent but her mouth did not tighten as it usually does when we talk about never returning home again. Just then the baby began to cry and Janet moved to pick her up.

"Here," Mother said. "I'll hold her for a while." She reached out her arms and Janet placed the baby in them. The baby quietened immediately. I was stunned. And then – oh my dear journal, how my heart glows to write this down – and then, I heard my mother sing. Softly, quietly, an old Scottish lullaby. The stitches blurred before my eyes and I had to duck my head so that no one would see the tears that suddenly flooded my eyes. A few dropped in spite of myself, but I do not think they did the quilt any harm.

I am being called. I will finish this tonight in bed.

Later

It is night now and I am tucked into my bed, with a tallow wick to give me light. Jamie is snoring companionably beside me.

Now I can write about the rest of the bee.

When we had finished quilting, we tidied everything up and all headed for a sort of community hall that has been built here for our gatherings, carrying the pots and dishes of food we had brought with us. The men and boys were waiting for us there. We served the supper. Then, no sooner had the dishes been emptied and the tables pushed back, but the fiddlers began to play and the dancing began. The whole hall was packed and shaking. I really did believe the walls would fall down. But what fun! Hannah and I danced together until her mother made her stop, then we just sat and watched the others. Her sister Molly was obviously popular with the young men there, but she didn't seem to favour any one over another. Hannah whispered to me that Molly kept talking about Angus and hoping that she will see him again when we all meet up in the spring. Hannah thinks she is besotted with him.

Grannie was mightily pleased when Uncle Allan Ross said her squirrel stew was the tastiest dish there. And then, would you believe it — he had *her* up to dance, too! I've never seen her so spry!

My wick is about to go out. I think I will just lie here in the dark and remember every moment of the day and night.

I was happy again. I was really, truly happy! I did not think that would ever be possible.

April 10th, 1784

Spring has definitely arrived! The birds are nesting, the sun is warm warm warm! I saw robins today.

April 14th, 1784

The ice on the river is beginning to break up. Mr. Mitchell is having a terrible time trying to keep order in school. We all have spring fever!

And what do you think — we have moved Grannie's lilac bush outside and there are fat green buds on it! It has survived!

April 26th, 1784

The river is almost open now and we are to leave next month. We are to be taken in boats up the St. Lawrence, past Montréal, to a town called Lachine. There we will transfer into more *bateaux* and set off farther upriver. (If it is one boat it is a *"bateau."* If it's more than one it's *"bateaux."* Father taught me that. There. Do you see, my journal? I am writing in French!) The families of the men and officers of Sir John Johnson's Regiment will be established in a new settlement which has been called Johnstown in his honour. They say it should take us about ten days to get there.

I am so excited!

April 30th, 1784

A letter from Angus! The first we have heard from him since the winter. He says all is well with him and he is looking forward to seeing us all again, but he was terribly sad to hear the news about baby Margaret. His battalion will be disbanded in June at Cataraqui and then he will be free to join us at Johnstown.

Mother got very quiet when she read his words about Margaret, but she is so happy at the thought of seeing Angus again. I begin to hope that she has even resigned herself to the fact that we will not be going home.

I wonder if Duncan will go to Johnstown as well?

May 2nd, 1784

We are to be out of here by May 10th. After that all supplies will be cut off and this camp will be closed. I cannot say that I will be sorry to see the last of it. A sorry, grimy place it is.

Mr. Mitchell has given up trying to hold classes. The boys have all deserted and those of us who are left are far too agog to settle down to lessons.

May 5th, 1784

Next week. We go next week!

May 9th, 1784

Tomorrow! We are packing what little we have and this small cabin is in a turmoil. I know I will not sleep a wink tonight.

May 12th, 1784

Lachine, near Montréal

We have come as far as Lachine and here we sit, waiting for boats to take us upriver to the Johnstown settlement. The river still has some ice in it and the trip so far has been frightening. At one point I thought the small boat we were packed into would founder. One boatman had to fend off huge chunks of ice with a pole while the other rowed with all his might. The current is fierce.

There are thousands of people gathered here, from military settlements as far downriver as Québec City, and the confusion, noise and general disarray is truly alarming.

Jamie and the Ross boys, of course, are doing their best to add to it. How three small boys can get into so much trouble I do not know. They disappeared for most of the afternoon and had us all looking frantically for them. We only found them because I heard Laddie barking. They had been searching for garter snakes — George wanted one as a pet — and had managed to get themselves away over on the other side of the encampment. They did find one poor unfortunate snake sunning on a rock but Laddie barked at it (that's when I heard him) and scared it away. That at least was a mercy. I cannot see trying to carry a snake along with us!

Laddie, by the way, was very unhappy at having to travel in a boat again. He just sat all hunched up between Jamie's feet with his ears drooping and his tail between his legs. He can look more mournful than any other dog I've ever seen.

May 14th, 1784

Still here and it would seem that we will be here for quite a while longer. I do not know how we will stand it. Father is worried, too, because we have only been issued with supplies for a month, although we have been assured that more supplies will follow us. They did give him ammunition, though, so he will be able to hunt. We had been promised more clothing, too, but it seems that the difficulties of distributing clothing are too great. I really do not understand that. I only understand that I have but one threadbare dress and my coat is in tatters. My stockings have been darned and mended until they are stiff. My boots will surely not last another month. Everyone else is in the same straits.

There are not enough boats assembled yet. Captain Jacob Maurer is in charge and he has been busy all winter, so we have been told, building *bateaux* and procuring other boats from wherever he can find them. Meanwhile, we all live in tents issued to us by the army. We have only one tent for our whole family. It is large, but at night the five of us are quite squashed up together. We don't really mind because the nights are still cold. Mother makes Laddie sleep outside, though, and Jamie is not happy about that.

Hannah and her family are right beside us this time.

May 16th, 1784

Grannie's little lilac bush has bloomed! Only one small spray of blossoms, but that spray is large enough that the spindly stem it is on is bent almost to the ground. I just shut my eyes and bury my nose in the deep purple blossoms and inhale great wafts of their smell, and for a moment or two I can almost believe I am home and all of this has just been one long bad dream.

But then I have to open my eyes.

May 18th, 1784

I am too cold and wet to write much. It has been raining constantly, with the result that we have had no fire and have had to make do with cold johnnycake and salt pork to eat. The mud all around our camp is so deep that we cannot move around very much. Just going over to Hannah's tent today I got the remains of my boots so muddy that Grannie made me take them off before I came into the tent. Even that did not help as my boots are so full of holes that my feet were just as filthy.

Grannie fights against dirt and mud constantly but I do not think she will win.

May 20th, 1784

Some Indian men came into camp today and brought fresh fish. They wanted to trade for flour but of course none of us had any to spare. They left the fish anyway, which I think was very kind of them.

The rain has stopped. Father built a lovely fire. I collected dandelion greens for a salad and Mother boiled fish with potatoes and turnips and some of Grannie's herbs. The turnips were a little mouldy but I cut the bad parts off and we had a wonderful feast.

May 21st, 1784

Some of the men who will be sailing the boats in which we will go upriver got drinking and wild last night. They are getting as impatient as we are. Grannie made Jamie and me go into our tent and stay there. She wouldn't even let me out to go into the bush to relieve myself until I convinced her that it was *absolutely* necessary! Then Jamie declared he had to go, too, and Mother said we couldn't go alone, and Father said he had better keep a watch out, so it was a regular parade into the bushes to the latrine. With Laddie bouncing around us and barking his big head off too, of course.

Very embarrassing.

May 25th, 1784

Finally! The boats are ready and are being loaded. It is reassuring to see all the supplies that are being sent along with us. As I write this, sitting on the riverbank and watching all the commotion, I can see the soldiers loading on tents and bales of cloth (a new dress this summer perhaps?) and hoes and axes and other tools. Boxes of provisions as well, and seed for planting, although Father, who is standing beside me, is worried that we will not be settled in time to plant our crops this year.

We leave tomorrow.

May 30th, 1784

Somewhere on the St. Lawrence River

This is the first chance I have had to write in my journal since we left. What a journey this is turning out to be!

The *bateau* in which we are travelling is like the one we sailed Lake Champlain in, but flat-bottomed to make it easier to drag through the rapids. Which we had to do immediately after setting off from Lachine. I will write of *that* later.

The *bateau* is manned by five sailors, as was the Lake Champlain one, but these men are French-Canadians. We say "*Bon jour*" to them every morning. That means "Good morning."

Again, we are packed in so tightly there is scarce room to breathe. As before, there are four families in the boat — including the Rosses, thanks be — and all our belongings. It is a mercy that we do not have much. There are twelve other *bateaux* travelling with us in a kind of brigade. All of us are families of men in Sir John Johnson's

Regiment and we will settle together. That is reassuring because we have gotten to know each other well over the past winter.

At night we come onshore and make our camp. It is really quite pleasant after the dirt and confusion of the camp at Lachine. As I sit here I am warmed by the fire and can see the boatmen cooking our dinner. One of them shot a brace of squirrels and the stew they are making smells wonderful. The weather has turned warmer, which is good in one way, but bad in another. The insects have begun to torment us. They are just as bad here as they were back home. Tiny black flies manage to get into my hair, my ears, down the neck of my dress — everywhere! And how they bite! I am scratching as much as writing at the moment. For shelter we have boat sails and tarpaulins slung over branches, but as long as it doesn't rain they are sufficient.

The sound of the river is in my ears as I write and I can see the moonlight shining off its waters. It is very beautiful.

June 1st, 1784

The boatmen sing constantly as we go along. Even though the boats have sails, they mostly have to row because the wind is against us from the west and we are going into a very strong current.

This is actually a very pleasant way to travel. Except for the insects. When we put in to shore for our noon meal we are immediately attacked by the black flies and mosquitoes, and the flies descend in such droves to cover our food that it is hard to take a bite without crunching down on one of them.

June 3rd, 1784

More rapids today. We have just finished going through them and are camped for our noon meal. The boatmen have made a huge bonfire in order to dry out, as several of them got very wet. One of the men slipped and fell right into the water and I heard him shout out something that I suspect might have been a swear word. Perhaps it is just as well that I haven't learned *too* much French!

The first time we went through rapids I was quite frightened, certain that all the boats were going to be lost. It is still frightening, but so far we have managed without mishap. Now I'll describe how it is done.

When we reach the beginning of the rapids, we passengers all disembark and take whatever is most precious to us, in case one of the boats does tip. These items we have to carry. There is a man called a conductor who is in charge of all the boats. His duty is to give directions for the safe management of the boats and keep them together whilst we are on the river. When we come to a rapids he directs the passage of the boats through, one by one. Two men stay in each boat to pole it. The others get out and walk along the shore and pull the boat through with ropes. The other Loyalist men help as well, and Father is always right in there with them.

The reason it is so frightening is because the rapids are so very powerful. I cannot help but fear for the safety of the men in the boats. If a boat ever tipped the man would be thrown into the rushing water and surely dashed to pieces on the rocks. One of the boats almost tipped today. We all stood with our hearts in our mouths until the men got it under control again.

They are brave men, those sailors.

They are distributing our bowls of soup now. I will have to stop writing.

Later

A near disaster! After our noon meal the boatmen began to load the boats up again and we began to gather up our possessions and take them down to the shore. No one noticed that the bonfire was spreading. All of a sudden there was a great outcry from one of the boatmen and we all rushed to see the fire racing through the leaves on the ground and heading for the forest.

Everyone grabbed up tarpaulins, blankets, anything they could reach, and began beating at the flames. I even beat at them with my blanket until Grannie saw me and pulled me away. Thank goodness the ground is not too dry yet and the flames were soon under control. I was quite sooty, but well pleased with myself. It was a very satisfying feeling to batter out that fire.

June 7th, 1784

Johnstown!

Well, we are here. I can hardly believe it. Johnstown is no more than a collection of tents strewn along the riverside. We have been given two. Father and Mother share a small one, Jamie, Grannie and I share the larger. (And Laddie, when Grannie is not looking.) The Rosses, as usual, are close beside us.

About twenty families are to settle here; the rest have continued upriver. Mr. Mitchell went with them. He is going to Cataraqui where there is already a school built. I will not miss him, but I wonder how long it will be until a school is built here? There is nothing at all so far.

I am being called. I must help with supper.

Everyone is strangely quiet. We are tired, of course, but I think it is more than that. Our long journey is finally over. What will happen now?

June 10th, 1784

Food is being distributed, but no clothing yet. I don't care. It was beautifully warm today and Hannah and I raced along the riverbank in just our old dresses and our bare feet. Who needs boots now?

Mother is busy organizing the food and supplies that we have been given, but every once in a while she just stops and gazes out at the forest all around us with a despairing look. Last night I heard her ask Father, "How, Robert, are we ever to make our home here? It is nothing but a wilderness!"

Father tried to reassure her, but it did not seem to help. It is hard to believe that this wild place can ever be home.

June 12th, 1784

They are surveying the land. When they are finished, Father says, all the families will draw lots for which piece of land we will own. As the head of a family, Father will get 100 acres, and Angus will get another 100 acres as well because he was a soldier. The rest of us in the family will also get 50 acres each, including Jamie and me. Uncle Allan will be entitled to 200 acres because he is a non-commissioned officer. It sounded very generous to me, but Mother had something to say about that.

"Generous indeed," she burst out. "When we have lost everything we owned, everything we ever worked for all these years because of our allegiance to Britain? And my baby — "

She broke off. I reached out to her but before I could say anything she gave herself a shake and straightened up. Her mouth got all grim looking.

"We've earned everything Britain can give us," she said. I had not thought of it that way. It made me feel sad all over again.

Father, Uncle Andrew and Uncle Allan are scouting out the woods each day. They would like to get adjoining lots and are looking for someplace with a stream running near it. I supposed Duncan would be entitled to 100 acres, too, and I suggested to Father that he look for a lot near us for him. Now Father is teasing me mercilessly, saying that I must be sweet on him. What nonsense! I was only thinking of Duncan's friendship with Angus.

June 14th, 1784

Father is worrying. The summer is wearing on and they have not yet finished surveying the lots. It will surely be too late to plant crops by the time we are settled. We will have to depend on Government supplies for the winter, Father says. He hates that!

June 21st, 1784

The wait grows wearisome. There is nothing for us to do. Hannah and I amuse ourselves by exploring along the river shore, but Father and the others are fretting about the delay.

Grannie, of course, is never idle. She is out early every morning replenishing her supply of roots and herbs. This morning she took Hannah and me along as well.

"High time you girls learned about these things," she said.

It is very interesting. Some plants will not be ready for picking until September or October, Grannie says, but there are many that we can harvest now. You would never know what is growing wild out there if you didn't have someone like Grannie to show you. I will make a list of the ones I know:

Spikenard for coughs and colds.

Bloodroot for sore noses.

Catnip for stomachache or sore throat.

Tansy tea as a tonic. (I know this one too well. It tastes *terrible!* Grannie thinks the worse a medicine tastes the better it is for you.)

Hop tea for regulating the blood. (How do you "regulate the blood"? What in the world does that mean? I asked Grannie, but she just shushed me.)

Black alder mixed with lard, resin and beeswax for scalds and burns. (I've had enough of those!)

Smartweed steeped in vinegar for bruises and swellings. (That's what we put on Jamie's head when he slid off the roof.) Sometimes wormwood is used instead. Especially for the legs of horses. I remember we used that once on old Blue.

Now I'm remembering old Blue and missing him.

Back to the herbs:

Burdock, a weed that mother detested because it insisted on invading her kitchen garden. Grannie steeped the dried leaves of it and gave it to Mother whenever she had indigestion, though, and it always seemed to help, so I suppose it could not be all bad.

Spearmint tea and mullein tea for colds.

Elecampane for open wounds. When made into a syrup it is supposed to help children suffering from whooping cough. (Thanks be we have not had need of that in this family.)

There is also something called nerve-vine. Grannie once tried to get me to chew the roots of it to "quieten my nerves," but I managed to talk her out of it by promising to be exceptionally quiet without it. (I don't believe I have *nerves*!)

And back to wormwood. Grannie makes a tea out of it that she gives to us if all else fails. It is so bitter it makes tansy tea taste sweet! When I smell wormwood tea brewing I take myself off no matter how sickly I feel.

June 23rd, 1784

Good news from Angus! His battalion is being disbanded and he will be here with us before the end of the month.

He didn't mention Duncan.

June 30th, 1784

Angus is here, and so is Duncan! Mother is smiling again and even Grannie is in a good mood. Father says they will be drawing the lots very soon and it is *about time!*

I have had a wonderful surprise — Angus brought me a kitten! She is all black with white paws so I have named her Mittens. She is the tiniest thing I have ever seen, but very brave. Laddie had to sniff her over as soon as he saw her, of course, and you would think she would have been afraid of such a huge monster — she isn't even as big as his head — but no such thing. When his sniffing grew a bit too rough, she just arched her back, ruffled up all her fur, spat at him like a little fury, and scratched his nose. He was so surprised! Jamie was most upset and certain that she had hurt Laddie. I found that very amusing, given the difference in their sizes, but I must admit that the dog has been giving her a wide berth ever since. She is curled up on my lap right now, purring away. Amazing that such a loud purr can come forth from such a small animal! It makes writing quite difficult, but I certainly don't care. It is just so grand to have such a warm, furry little thing to cuddle. I let Hannah hold her, too, of course, and Mother is quite taken with her.

July 2nd, 1784

We are all registering for land but there is much skullduggery afoot. It seems that some people are very greedy. Father says that some officers have been registering their children as officers so that they may receive a larger grant. One man registered his month-old baby as a major, and another registered his two dogs as his sons!

Mittens has decided she wants to play with Laddie. He is very worried about it. I think he fears for his nose.

July 8th, 1784

Finally! The drawing of the lots will be done today. It is very hard to wait.

Mittens is curled up asleep between Laddie's paws. I think he thinks he is her mother now. It is most amusing to watch them together. She pounces on his tail when he is sleeping and he jumps up, ready to do battle, then gets all soft and loony when he sees it's just the kitten. I would never have believed he could be so gentle.

Later

What a day! This settling of lots was a very complicated affair involving a lot of noise and shouting. At one point it seemed that two men might even come to blows when they could not agree on a fair trade.

This is how it was done. The men drew pieces of paper with numbers of lots out of a hat and then the surveyor entered their lot numbers upon the map that he had drawn. Then everyone started swapping and trading around in order to get the particular lots they wanted. I don't think I drew breath until we found out which one we would get. The officers got to draw first and got all the land fronting upon the river. After much conniving, Uncle Andrew and Uncle Allan managed to get land near ours. Angus managed to get a lot right next to ours, and Duncan was finally able to swap for a lot nearby as well. It took a whole day of bargaining and bartering and Father is exhausted, but we are all well pleased. There is a good stream going through all our properties and Father says that is a blessing. It will provide us with water without the need for a well right away.

July 9th, 1784

I wonder if life will ever settle down to comfortable boredom again? The whole camp is in confusion and we are packing up all our belongings for yet one more time. We have been given generous rations from the government supplies, and with Angus and Duncan to help we will be able to carry everything, although they might have to make more than one trip. I hope it is not too far.

We are about to leave. Mother is calling me. Hannah and her family left earlier. Even though they will be settling near us, I am sore afraid it will be quite some time before I see her again. I noticed that Angus and Molly took a long time to make their farewells. It would seem Angus is as interested in her as she is in him.

Hmmm. I wonder how I would like having bossy Molly as a sister-in-law? But then, Hannah would also be my sister-in-law. That would be wonderful.

I must go. Grannie is chivvying me along. Angus has given me the cage he brought Mittens in to carry her in. She does not like it one bit and Laddie keeps sniffing at it and looking up at me with a decidedly anxious look. He seems to be wondering why we have imprisoned her.

July 10th, 1784

No time to write, there is too much to do. I will tell all about what has happened tomorrow. Also, I am very *very* tired. We walked our feet off today.

Cold salt pork and johnnycake for supper, but at least we are *here*. Even though I am not entirely certain where *here* is. It is certainly dark and lonely! I am keeping Mittens in the tent with me for fear of wild animals.

July 11th, 1784

We have set up our tents in a small clearing that Father and the boys made, with a huge bonfire burning in the middle. Angus and Duncan shot four squirrels today and Mother is making a squirrel stew. The smell of it is making my mouth water, although I am almost too tired to eat. I am sitting in front of our tent. Grannie's lilac bush is beside me. It has finished blooming of course, but is now covered with glossy green leaves and looks very satisfied with itself. As well it should. A hardy little thing to have survived all it has survived.

We're all pretty hardy, as a matter of fact. But worn out.

Mittens is attacking a leaf with great ferocity.

Now I'll write about our trip here yesterday.

We left the encampment at Johnstown very early in the morning, well loaded down with our tents and supplies. Thank goodness we had Angus and Duncan with us as they could carry an enormous amount. Even so, they will have to make one or two trips more.

Right away we ran into trouble. Father had scouted out the land fairly well, but he was not certain of the exact location of the lots which we had been assigned. There were no roads, just tracks through the bush, and nothing really to indicate the boundary lines, but finally after much searching we managed to find the markers placed by the surveyors. By this time, however, it was almost evening and we were exhausted from trying to find our way through the dense woods. There was no time to rest, though. We dumped our packs onto the ground and Father unpacked the axes. Great consternation when he discovered the axes we have been issued are small ships' axes and not nearly as suitable for the hard work we have in store for us as the larger ones he is used to. There was nothing to be done for it however, but to use them.

Father, Angus and Duncan set to work cutting down trees and brush to make a clearing large enough for our tents. It took them quite a while. I truly do not think I have ever seen so many trees. And the mosquitoes were terrible. Still are, despite the smoke from the fire. Finally we were able to set up the tents. Angus and Duncan have a small soldier's tent each, we have the two larger ones we were given at Johnstown.

We made a very hasty meal — as I described last night — and were soon into our tents and fast asleep. We only had tarpaulins thrown over fir boughs to sleep on, but not one of us even noticed, we were that exhausted.

This morning I was first up. I crept out of our tent, carrying a sleepy Mittens, and watched the sun rise. At least, I watched the sky lighten. There are so many trees I could not see the sun itself, just the straggly rays that managed to find their ways down through the branches.

I had a lovely half hour before the mosquitoes woke up and I just sat there, listening to the birds awaken and breathing in great gulps of the fresh, pine-smelling air, with Mittens frolicking around me.

It was soothing to my soul.

July 12, 1784

Father, Angus and Duncan spent the day exploring our land, deciding where we will build our cabin. Angus and Duncan will help us get our place built, then they will build shanties of their own on their properties.

Father brought us here to see the site he chose this afternoon. It is on a small hillock, right beside the stream.

"Will it do, Fiona?" he asked Mother. He looked so anxious! Mother did not answer for a long moment and I held my breath. She looked around, then back at him.

"It will, Robert," she answered finally. "It is a good spot."

I let out my breath with such a huge sigh that I was certain they must have heard it, but they just stood there, looking at each other. Then Mother gave herself a kind of shake and pursed her lips.

"But I shudder to think of the work ahead of us," she said. "And so little time before winter sets in."

Father's face cleared and he smiled a huge smile. He put his arm around Mother's shoulders. "We can do it, Fiona," he said. His voice suddenly sounded ten times stronger than it has since we left Albany.

I saw Mother relax then. She even rested her head on his shoulder.

"Yes," she said. "I suppose we can."

It's been so long since I've seen them like this with each other. Oh, how I hope this means Mother is starting to accept our new life. I don't care how much work it is going to be, I just want us to be happy again!

I'm sitting on the very spot where we will build, right now as I write this, and tomorrow we will start to clear the land.

I close my eyes and I can hear the water rushing along the stream bed, gurgling and rippling its way over stones and around bends. I will have this sound in my ears for the rest of my life!

Oof! Laddie has just run up to shake himself off all over me. He has been swimming in the creek. Mittens has retreated to a safe distance, thoroughly disgusted.

I will probably have the smell of wet dog in my nose for the rest of my life, too.

July 13th, 1784

We attacked the forest today. All of us except for Grannie, who stayed to tend the fire and cook a very welcome meal for us.

There were axes enough for all of us except for Jamie of course. Father would not allow Jamie to use one, much to his disgust, but set him to collecting the branches as we chopped, and piling them up. It did not take me long to learn how to wield an axe. Mother showed me how. I was surprised to see how expert she was.

"This is not the first home I have helped to build," she said. "I was just about your age when I helped my parents build theirs." Then she laid to and soon had a small tree down and in pieces. I joined her. It was hard work. Harder work than I've ever done in my life. When we stopped to make our way back and eat the fried pork and johnnycake Grannie had ready for us, my shoulders and arms were aching. Not nearly as much as they are aching now, though, even though Grannie gave me a good rubbing with her smartweed concoction.

We went back to work after our dinner and worked through until the day began to darken. We are all stiff and sore, and Mother and I have huge blisters on our hands, but when I look at how much we have cleared I am filled with a great sense of pride and accomplishment. I think we all feel the same. Mother was even humming again under her breath as she set out fresh-baked bread and cold salt pork.

July 16th, 1784

We have cleared enough space for our cabin and a small garden. I am helping Mother hoe it but the ground is so hard and so packed with roots that we are having a very hard time of it. We have used some of the brush and smaller trees to make a fence around the garden to keep out deer and other wild animals, but there is nothing to be done about the stumps that are left, so we are just scratching around them. Father was right to worry about the lateness of the season. It is much too late now to plant corn or potatoes, but Mother says we might get some beans and turnips in. She is definitely getting her old enthusiasm back. Her "get up and go," as Grannie calls it.

We will start clearing land for wheat and corn and flax next year. Grannie will be able to spin tow thread out of the flax. I will help her — that has been my job since I was Jamie's age. Her hands are too old now to soak the stalks of flax and beat them, so I do that for her. Even for me that's hard work. I do that and then pull them through the hatchel to comb the stalks out and just leave the fibre, then Grannie spins it. Then we can take it to a weaver. If we're lucky and if she has her new loom by then, it will be Aunt Norah. (The Livingstones are settled right in the town — or what will be the town — of Johnstown.) I suppose Aunt Norah will mostly mix the tow thread with wool to make itchy linsey-woolsey for clothes, but I do hope we will have enough so that she can just weave the flax thread all by itself. That makes a lovely soft linen. Our curtains back home were made from that.

Father has helped me pick out a spot for my apple seeds and I planted them carefully. It will be years before the trees will be big enough to bear fruit, but I can wait.

Father has piled all the brush up and we will burn it sometime, but not now. It is too dry now and Father says a bonfire would be dangerous. After seeing how quickly that fire spread when we were on our way here, even when the ground was still wet, I can certainly agree.

Father, Angus and Duncan will begin building the cabin tomorrow.

My hands are an agony. I'm sure Mother's are the same but she does not complain, so neither will I. We slather them with Grannie's ointments.

July 17th, 1784

There will be no cellar or foundation for this cabin, but Angus and Duncan dug a small excavation which will be reached through a trap door in the cabin floor, by means of a ladder, and we will use that as a root cellar for the time being. They have also helped Father place boulders at each corner of the building to give support for the walls. It was difficult to roll the boulders into place without a horse to pull them, but Angus and Duncan managed to do so with ropes and levers. They are very clever. Angus says they learned how to do this over the winter when they were working at Cataraqui with the army. Angus is so enthusiastic about starting out all over again here in Canada. I asked him if he didn't miss Albany at all and he just said, "Not a bit." I don't really believe him, but I guess he sure wouldn't want to go back after having fought on the British side. There wouldn't be anyone left who wouldn't hate him. I have no idea how Duncan feels but I don't dare ask him. He works as willingly as Angus, but he does not seem to be as happy.

We are really lucky to have them both helping us, though. It makes things a lot easier.

I like to look at those four boulders and imagine a nice snug cabin built on top of them. I hope Father will put in windows.

July 18th, 1784

It's Sunday today so we did no work on the cabin. I could see that Father was chafing at the inactivity when there is so much to do, but in this Grannie will have her way. I am hiding out of her sight in order to write this, and Angus disappeared after the noon meal. I would not be surprised at all if he is doing a bit of clearing at his place. Do you suppose we are being very sinful, dear journal?

July 19th, 1784

The real work begins today. Father and the boys have started cutting pine trees for the logs for the walls. They have to fell the trees, then cut them into proper lengths and hew them into shape. There is not much Mother and Jamie and I can do to help them with that, but we can help them pull the logs over to the cabin site. The logs are very heavy and it takes all of our strength together to move them. I did not think I could get any sorer or stiffer, but I have.

July 21st, 1784

The walls are starting to go up! Father says he will make them high enough so that there will be a loft for Jamie and me to sleep in. And Jamie and I found a patch of raspberries growing wild in an open spot nearby. Raspberries are my very favourite and they seem to be Laddie's favourite as well. Jamie gave him a few. At first he seemed at a loss as to what to make of them, then he decided he liked them. Jamie wasn't giving them to him fast enough, however, so he began nibbling them off the bushes himself. It was very amusing to see him nip them off so delicately, one by one. And he seems very adept at avoiding the thorns. Better than I am, anyway. My hands and arms are thoroughly scratched right up to my elbows. We managed to bring home a whole bucket full, though. Now — if we only had good thick cream to pour over them!

July 23rd, 1784

It is beginning to seem as if we have never done anything else but hew logs, drag them around, and work. We are up at sunrise and fall into our beds when the sun goes down. We are too tired even to talk. Father barely stops for a break at noon time. He is worrying more and more that we will not have time to build a cabin and then bring in any crops at all to help us through the winter that is to come.

"We must have good shelter and at least some food of our own," he says. "We cannot depend entirely on the Government for all our supplies."

Then Jamie gave us all a scare by deciding that he, too, should be able to chop wood. Before anyone realized what he was doing, he had hoisted an axe and aimed a mighty blow at one of the logs. Of course he was not nearly strong enough. The axe glanced off the log and grazed his foot. Cut through his boot and nicked him. There was a tremendous amount of blood for such a small cut and he thought he was dying. Mother didn't wait for Grannie — she laid into him with a switch herself.

Father was furious. "Is it not enough that we have only a few short months to prepare ourselves for winter?" he thundered. "We cannot *afford* accidents." I have seldom seen him so angry. I think it is the worry that is doing it.

Thank goodness for Grannie's hearty meals every night and good breakfasts in the mornings. My hands are so calloused and rough that it hurts me to help her wash up after, though. Grannie rubs goose grease into them, but it does not help much. I would certainly not be able to do much stitching on a quilt now.

July 24th, 1784

We found weevils in the flour this morning. I was given the job of picking them out. Weevily or not, we will have to use it. That is the only flour we have until we receive more supplies. *If* we receive more supplies. That is the fear that is in the back of Father's mind, I am sure.

July 26th, 1784

What a terrible day! I am still shaking as I write this. Jamie and I found a blueberry patch today in a rocky clearing near the river's edge. I knew we had strayed too far from home, but the day was so fine and I was in an exploring mood. Mother had sent us berry picking and I was so relieved to have a rest from work. When we stumbled upon the blueberry patch we immediately set to picking and I lost all sense of time.

"Isn't it getting late, Mary?" Jamie suddenly asked me.

I looked up at the sky. We live in trees so much of the time that I am used to it being dark and shadowy, but I suddenly realized that the sun had left the clearing where we were and was far down in the sky. Our pails were full and we had both eaten our fill as well, so we whistled to Laddie and made ready to come home. But Laddie did not appear and Jamie would not go without him. Jamie whistled and I called, but to no avail for the longest time. Then, suddenly, the dog burst out of a nearby clump of bushes, his tail between his legs and his eyes wild with fright. He ran up to Jamie and pressed himself against Jamie's legs, then turned to face the bushes again and growled. His fur was standing straight up along his back and his teeth were bared.

"Run, Jamie!" I shrieked, and we both lit out down the trail back to our campsite, Laddie at our heels. Then I heard a great crashing noise in the trees behind us.

A bear! It had to be a bear! Without really thinking about what I was doing, I threw my berry pail and all its contents onto the trail.

"Your berries, Jamie!" I shouted. "Throw him your berries."

Jamie did so, but he had sense enough to hang onto his pail.

We heard no more sounds of pursuit, but Laddie kept turning to growl and we ran as fast as our feet would take us until we were safely back.

Now Mother has forbidden us to go berry picking anywhere except right near the cabin, so I suppose that will mean no more blueberries for us, as they only grow in the cleared, rocky spots down near the river. I mourn the loss of blueberry pies. Angus said I should be mourning the loss of a perfectly good bucket, but he must have felt a little sorry for me as he was especially nice to me at supper time.

July 30th, 1784

There is so much work to do and I am so tired at night that I have not been writing in my journal as often as I would like. The cabin is beginning to take shape, however. There will be two small windows, Father says, one on either side of the door. He'll cut them out after the walls go up. He and the boys are putting in the rafters that will be the ceiling of the main floor, and the floor of the loft. Tomorrow he will start on the chimney. Jamie and I have been set to finding good flat stones to serve as the hearth and small sticks to be layered up with mud for the chimney itself. When it is finished Father says he will plaster it over with clay, inside and out.

August 2nd, 1784

It is hard to believe that summer is nearing its end. But we will have a snug cabin to live in for the winter.

"No wood floor this year, I'm afraid, Fiona," my

Father said, "but next year I'll put one in for you first thing."

Mother just shook her head.

"I can wait for my wood floor quite easily," she answered and gave Father a big smile. "It's a lovely cabin you're building for us, Robert."

Mother smiles a lot lately and is so much more like her old self. It makes me feel quite light inside.

Even though Mother and Father are working so hard, they are much happier than they were last winter. Not being able to *do* anything for all those long months was worse than having too much to do, I think. They are not used to being useless!

Now, as long as we get those supplies . . .

August 10th, 1784

The roof is going on today! Just bark for this year, but next year Father will make a better one. No glass for the windows, but oiled paper will do. No door, either, until Father gets a proper saw. We have sacrificed one of the blankets we were issued to hang in the doorway for now. I do hope we get a door before winter sets in!

Jamie and I are helping to chink the logs with sticks and moss, and Father will plaster them over with clay, too.

August 17th, 1784

The cabin is finished, and Father built a privy out back as well. No more treks into the dark woods at night, thank goodness. I always imagine all kinds of wild animals behind every bush whenever I have to go. The cabin looks so safe and cosy, nestled in under the trees. And just think, dear journal, I helped to build it! I even helped build the privy.

Angus and Duncan are now starting to build shanties of their own on their own properties, but until they are done they will continue to live in their tents.

Father is making furniture for us. He is building bunks against the walls for Jamie and me up in the loft, and two larger beds in the main room for Mother and himself and for Grannie. Mother has her feather tick that we carried all the way here, but the rest of us will have to do with blankets thrown over balsam fir and pine boughs, until we can harvest straw next summer or get corn husks next fall. Later on, when we have geese again, we will have feather ticks as well. That won't be for a while, though, I don't think.

Mother has also made a curtain out of the fabric that was supplied to us, that can be pulled across to give her and Father some privacy at night. (No new dress for me yet, I'm afraid.)

We will use stumps for tables and benches. Those dratted stumps do come in handy for some things.

Angus came by today to tell us how his shanty is coming along, and he brought us some dishes and spoons that he had whittled out of poplar wood. They are very welcome, as we only have a very few earthenware plates and bowls. Mother's precious china platter sits now on a shelf that Father made for it and she will only use it for special dinners.

Angus said that he and Duncan saw a bear yesterday. I wonder if it is the one that chased Jamie and me. Angus says if they see it again they are going to shoot it and we will have bear meat for the whole winter. I don't think it very wise for Angus to try to shoot a bear and I said so.

"Would that not be dangerous?" I asked him.

"I have shot beings far more dangerous, Mary," he answered and his face got suddenly all flat and grim.

He must have shot and killed many men during the war. Somehow I had never thought of that. My own brother. And Duncan, too. It is not something that I really want to think about.

Angus also brought some quill pens that Duncan whittled for me from some turkey buzzard feathers that he found. It seems Duncan has taken note of my habit of scribbling and thought I might be able to use them. That was thoughtful of him.

August 30th, 1784

We have moved into the cabin! Our own little house at last. It is nowhere near as roomy or as comfortable as our house back home, of course, but I cannot begin to describe how overjoyed I feel. The fire is burning brightly, Laddie is stretched out snoring before it, and Mittens is curled up right beside him, purring. This is a home indeed.

No sooner were we settled in than Grannie insisted on planting her lilac bush. Father dug a hole for it right beside our door stoop and I carried a bucket of water up from the stream to water it. The leaves haven't drooped a bit. It looks tiny and pathetic, but it also looks like it's there to stay. Just imagine, next spring we will have lilacs in the doorway again.

Mother made us a feast tonight, cooked in our own fireplace. Angus and Duncan shot a deer in the forest and we had the most delicious, sizzling, juicy roast of venison I have ever tasted. It was so good! Grannie made bread in our bake kettle. I sopped up every last bit of juice with it. We have no butter now but it did not even matter.

For dessert we had Lumpy Dick served on Mother's china platter, made with raspberries that Jamie and I picked. It was without a doubt the most wonderful meal that I have ever had in my life.

Before we ate we all joined hands around the table and gave thanks to God for all we have. It is much, and we are very fortunate to have been able to get here safely.

September 6th, 1784

What a surprise today. I was digging away at the garden, fighting those dratted roots and saying words under my breath that I wouldn't want Grannie to hear, when Laddie began to bark furiously. I looked up and there were two Indians! We knew there were Indian villages near here, but so far we have seen no sign of the Indians themselves. We had been assured that they were friendly, however, and willing to share their land with us, so we were not frightened when these two appeared. Father tried to talk to them, but they are from the Mississauga tribe and Father does not know their language. They made clear what they had come for, however. They tossed sacks onto the ground and took out ears of fresh corn. They obviously wanted to trade and this time we were able to do so. Mother gave them a sackful of our flour. They didn't seem to mind the weevils. Then, realizing I suppose that we had no means of grinding the corn, they showed Father how to hollow out the top of a stump and grind the corn in that with a stone fastened onto a long pole for leverage.

We will have a grist mill on the river here next spring, it seems, but this will have to do until then.

Father seemed to get on very well with them. I do not know how he managed to understand them, but he tells us that they will take him fishing on the river tomorrow night. They have huge canoes that hold around ten men, and they use a flaming torch called a jack light at the bow to attract the fish. They spear the fish with long spears. Father is very excited about it all. How I would love to go too, but I know better than to even suggest it. I suppose Duncan and Angus will go, though.

September 7th, 1784

Father came home with a basket full of fish last night and we had boiled fish for dinner. He says he will go out with the Indians again so we will have a good supply of fresh fish from now on and we can salt some down for the winter. He says they are going to show him how to make moccasins, too, out of the deerskins we have — after he tans them — so we will have shoes for our feet this winter.

What fun to wear Indian moccasins! Much nicer than heavy old boots.

It makes it a little less worrisome to know that we will have a good supply of fish and game laid in for the winter, even if we won't have too many crops.

September 13th, 1784

Just when things were beginning to go well — how could I be so stupid! I was helping Mother with the washing and tipped the pot of boiling water over. Some of it splashed onto my leg and burned it badly. I am sitting here with my leg wrapped up in cloths and Grannie's black alder ointment smeared all over it, but it still hurts so much that I cannot stop weeping. The only good thing is that Mittens leaped out of the way just in time. I could not have borne it if I had burned her as well.

I thought writing in my journal would help, but it isn't helping a bit. I'll try to write later on.

September 14th, 1784

My leg is still unbelievably painful but we had the best surprise today. It cheered me up no end in spite of myself.

Mother was working in her garden this morning and Father was busy clearing as usual. Angus was over helping, although there is still much to be done on his own lot. He had just helped me out to the front stoop to sit in the sun and keep an eye on Jamie, and for once he didn't even tease me about anything — I think he actually feels quite sorry for me — when suddenly we heard the noise of horse's hooves. We couldn't believe it, but sure enough, out of the trees came a horse and rider. It was Uncle Allan Ross! He came to bring us news of his family and to see how we were. I have never been so pleased to see anyone in my life. I could not stop my tongue from wagging, asking him how Hannah was, did her family have their cabin built yet, and a thousand other questions, not to mention, how did he ever get a horse and from where? Grannie said it was fortunate that I could not move from where I was put or I would probably have been jumping all over the poor man. And I probably would have.

Anyway, he told us that Uncle Andrew and Aunt Norah have built a cabin much like ours, and Hannah is fine. He is living with them until he gets his own cabin built. Hannah sent me a note and I have it here beside me. I keep reading it and reading it. She writes just the way she talks — her sentences ramble on and on and just run into each other and never seem to stop. Oh how I do miss her!

Uncle Allan and Father have organized a logging bee and it is to be held here. They and some of the other men will help us clear more acreage, and girdle the trees too big to chop down, by cutting a strip of bark out all around them, so they will die over the winter. It has been raining quite a bit lately so they feel the woods are in no danger if we start burning all the brush and trees that we have already felled. They will all come here in a week or so, then Father and the boys will go to the Rosses' place, and then on to the other neighbours who join in after that. It will be a busy fall.

Best of all, Uncle Allan has told me that Hannah and her family will come, too.

Uncle Allan not only managed to procure a horse, but he tells us he has a wagon as well. They are going to try and widen the path through the forest so that he can bring it through. That will help with the work, and he says he has been given provisions to bring to us as well! Governor Haldimand has kept his word and a whole new load of supplies arrived in Johnstown to be distributed amongst all the settlers. Father's face lightened as if the worries of the world had been lifted from his shoulders at that news.

September 15th, 1784

All other work has stopped and Father and Angus and Duncan are bending their efforts toward making a road. The air rings with the sound of their axes from morning until evening. They don't even stop for a meal at noon time, just eat what bits of bread and cheese they take with them in the morning. At least they have better axes to work with. Uncle Allan Ross brought them some good big double-headed axes.

I suppose Uncle Allan and Uncle Andrew are working away just as hard from their end. Soon we will have a proper road joining us to the Rosses and then, I hope, we'll get a road all the way into Johnstown. Uncle Allan said that they have built a church and Mr. Murchison preaches there on Sundays. It would be so good to be able to go — we would feel so much less alone if we could meet with our neighbours once in a while.

Uncle Allan had all sorts of news to tell us. It seems that Johnstown is growing by leaps and bounds. There are several proper houses there now, as well as the church. They are even planning a school for next year. Wouldn't it be wonderful if they asked Father to teach? With Mr. Mitchell off in Cataraqui, I don't see where they could find anyone else. I think the thought has crossed Father's mind, too, as he looked very pensive when Uncle Allan mentioned it.

September 20th, 1784

My leg is much better and I am able to hobble around now. It still hurts, though, and looks awful. All scabby and red. I suppose I will carry the scar with me for the rest of my life. At least no one but me sees my legs.

September 24th, 1784

We are beginning to prepare for the logging bee. We must have boundless quantities of food on hand. Mother and Grannie and I have been baking and boiling and cooking from morning till evening. Jamie, of course, is constantly underfoot and has his fingers in everything if we don't watch him. Grannie has rapped his knuckles more than once and she is getting exasperated. He had better watch out.

September 27th, 1784

The logging bee was today. What a vast amount of work, and what fun. Best of all, Hannah and her family brought their tent and are staying over. Mind you, Hannah is not sleeping in it. Mother gave permission for her to share my bed tonight. We have talked ourselves silly. I cannot begin to describe how happy I was to see her again. She is curled up beside me as I write and she has finally fallen asleep. My eyes want to close so much too, I am so tired, but I just had to write this down. I will tell of the bee tomorrow, and also of all the other good things that happened.

The house is full of people snoring!

September 28th, 1784

It was so hard to say goodbye to Hannah today, but now that we have a road joining our houses, I am certain we will see more of each other. At least until the snow comes.

Now to tell of all that happened.

First I will start with what Uncle Allan and Uncle Andrew brought us. When Uncle Allan said he had supplies for us, he didn't tell the half of it. Here is what he brought:

– more tools for Father, including a good saw (It will be most useful for cutting down the girdled

trees next spring, not to mention making a door!)
– more ammunition for Father's musket, which he sorely needs
– two scythes and a sickle to help us reap our harvest next year
– a frow for splitting shingles so that Father may make us a proper roof

Oh, and a host of other boring but necessary things.

Here is the best part:

He brought a spinning wheel for Grannie and two fleeces of wool! Grannie is beside herself. If there had not been so much to do today I warrant she would have been spinning away already.

And he brought chickens! A cage with several chickens and a rooster just for us! Father will make a chicken coop for them for the nights, because of the danger of foxes, but during the day they can peck around in the yard. I was worried that Mittens might chase them, but she is afraid of them. I am looking forward to an egg. I cannot remember the last time I tasted an egg.

Angus and Duncan came just about the same time as the Rosses and helped us unload their wagon. By the time we had it all done, the others began to arrive. It was such fun to see the people we had come to know at Machiche last winter. Some had wagons, some just came on foot. The men all brought axes and saws, the women brought food.

The Livingstones were all piled into one wagon and Mother and Mrs. Livingstone were so pleased to see each other again. Their baby is toddling all over the place now and Mother couldn't stop laughing at her.

The Calders came and Alex blushed scarlet red when he saw Hannah. She pretended not to even notice him, but her eyes got very bright and sparkly when she saw him, even though she denied it when I teased her about it.

The Stantons and the Hooples came too, and I was glad to see Annie and Flossie, though not as glad as I was to see Hannah. Mr. Snyder came with Danny. Danny is just as dimwitted as ever.

The men were all laughing and shouting to each other as they began to gather up all the brushwood and small trees that Father and Angus and Duncan had cut down. They made a huge pile of them and set it alight. What a bonfire it made! Then they set to clearing out more bush and trees.

Meanwhile, in the kitchen, Mother and Grannie and Hannah and I, and all the other women and girls, were busy cooking and baking. We knew those men would be hungry when they finished their work and my, were they ever! They worked right through until the early afternoon and so did we. The men burned all of the underbrush and small trees and the tops and branches of the larger trees they had cut down and left only the charred trunks of those trees to be disposed of. They chopped firewood enough for us to last the winter, and by the time they were done with the burning, they were all quite black with soot. Mother was very disapproving because a jug of whiskey appeared when they were finished and was being passed around quite liberally. Father abstained. I think the memory of the last time he drank whiskey was enough for him. Neither Angus nor Duncan would dare drink under my Mother's watchful eye, but several of the other men laid into it quite enthusiastically. Mr. Snyder got quite drunk and I wouldn't be surprised if that idiot Danny had not had a swig or two as well. He certainly seemed sillier than usual when it came time to wash up. We had set up logs and stumps to sit on in the clearing outside the cabin, and a vat of soft soap beside tubs of water which Hannah and I and the other girls had hauled up from the creek.

"Don't be so disapproving, Fiona," I heard Grannie say. "The men have worked hard and they need their reward. Just look at how much they've done for us."

There's also a huge vat of ashes to be made into

lye for soap and potash and to use in the privy. Not that the privy ever smells sweet, no matter how much lye we throw down into it, but it does help.

We brought out pots and pots of soup and squirrel and porcupine stew and fried salt pork, and those men ate everything as fast as we laid it on the table. We also had boiled fish that Father and the Indians had caught, and roasts from another deer that Uncle Andrew Ross had shot. Mrs. Livingstone and Aunt Norah had brought loaves and loaves of bread, and of course Grannie and Mother had been baking as well. We joined in when everything was set out and it turned into a real party.

When we were finished eating, Mr. Stanton brought out a fiddle and the dancing began. I saw Danny heading toward me, no doubt intending to ask me to partner him, but thanks be Duncan beat him to it and I made certain to avoid Danny from then on. I danced with Duncan until I was quite dizzy. Duncan is so courteous. He doesn't treat me at all like Angus's bothersome little sister. But there is something about him . . . Even when he's dancing, his mouth is laughing, but his eyes are sad. I wonder if it is more than just missing his family.

Angus and Molly never took their eyes off each other.

"I see a wedding in the spring," I heard Mrs. Livingstone say, and Mother and Aunt Norah smiled at each other.

A wolf is howling. How despairing he sounds, but tonight I do not feel lonely at all. I am just so glad to be in this warm and safe little house with my family all around me and knowing that good neighbours are close. Having a road to join us makes such a difference.

September 30th, 1784

Grannie is chipper and cheery. She is at her spinning wheel all day long. It is an even better one than the one she had in Albany, as she can sit down at it and it has a foot treadle for turning the wheel and a removable wooden bobbin. I am carding the fleeces for her so that they will be combed out, and she is spinning the wool. Jamie has been set to winding the wool onto the niddy noddy as she spins it. He's supposed to measure 40 lengths exactly around the frame, but I can tell that he does not always count correctly.

I can use a drop spindle of course, all girls can, but Grannie is going to teach me to use the spinning wheel as well. I will have wool to knit myself a good warm pair of mittens this winter. And Mother says she will teach me to knit socks. I have not yet mastered the art of turning a heel.

Father is making Mother a new quilting frame and Grannie says it is high time that I started making quilts for my marriage. For my marriage! What a thought! Fortunately I will have several years before *that* happens, but all girls should have at least two or three quilts done before then. I will either have to learn to stitch more quickly or delay my marriage for a long, long time.

It is going to be a busy winter. Not like the last one. Now if I could only go back to school I would be happy.

October 3rd, 1784

We were most surprised to see a man on horseback ride up the path to our house today. It was Mr. Murchison, our preacher, and as it was Sunday, he held services with us in our house. He will stay over the night and then go on and visit the other families as well. He brought news that the road will be through to the town next spring. There will be a sawmill and a grist mill there next spring as well, and the schoolhouse is almost finished. And . . . wait for it, dear journal . . . Father is being asked to be the schoolmaster! Mr. Murchison asked Father if he would consider it, but he hardly needed to pose the question. Father's face lit up like one of the German families' Christmas trees. He is bellowing out "The Golden Vanity" at the top of his voice even as I write this.

Oh, no he's not. Not now. Mr. Murchison just came in from outside and Father has switched quickly to a hymn. It sounds just as gleeful, though.

To make things even better, in payment Father will be given a cow, a pair of geese, two lambs and a piglet. What riches!

October 4th, 1784

Grannie and I picked herbs today. We will hang them in bunches by the fire to dry.

October 6th, 1784

I just wrote down the date and then realized it is exactly one year since I started this journal. One year since that dreadful day when they burned the schoolhouse down at our old home in Albany.

What a lot has happened since then. I do not even feel like the same girl. So much has happened. So much has changed. We have endured so much. The times ahead will be just as hard, I am certain of it, but I look around me and see a home and the beginnings of gardens and fields in what was, just a few short months ago, nothing but forest. And all around us there are other homes, other cabins and gardens and fields coming into being. I cannot see them but I can feel them. We are not alone. We have survived, we Loyalists. We are a sturdy folk.

Best of all, Mother confided in me just two minutes ago that we will have our own little "born Canadian" come next spring. We are here to stay.

October 7th, 1784

Angus came round early this morning and said he wanted us to go see the shanty he has built, so Mother packed a picnic lunch and off we went. Grannie did not go, but the rest of us did, Laddie too, of course. Mittens was off about her own business which was just as well as I didn't want her following us all that distance. She is getting quite independent and has turned into a very good mouser. Still a cuddly cat though when she feels like it. I'm glad of that because I do love to cuddle her.

When we got to Angus's shanty, Duncan was there waiting for us. It was nice to see him again. Angus's shanty is very small and has no windows at all. It is not much bigger than the coop Father built for our chickens and it only has a hole in the roof for the smoke to escape, instead of a proper chimney, but Angus is very proud of it. So he should be. It is snug and well-chinked and I'm sure he will be very comfortable in it this winter. Next summer, of course, he will have to build a proper cabin — especially if he is thinking of marriage. I don't dare ask him about that, though.

Duncan wanted us to go and see his shanty as well, but Mother had the picnic lunch all spread out and declared that she couldn't walk another step. I think she is beginning to be a bit tired because of the baby. Father was stretched out on his back, snoozing — just about the first time I've seen him so at ease since we settled here — and he was not about to move, so only Jamie and Laddie and I accompanied Duncan.

Duncan's shanty is much like Angus's, but he has put in one small window.

"I must have light," he said. I can understand that — it is exactly how I feel.

His shanty is on the same stream that runs through Angus's and our properties, but I think it is more prettily situated. It sits halfway up a little hill and the creek runs down behind it over a small waterfall. Duncan showed me all around with such pride. He even made Jamie and me a fine lunch of freshly caught fried fish from the stream and bread that he had baked himself. I've never known a man to bake bread! I was much impressed. We sat outside on a bench that he had made while we ate. Jamie was determined to catch a fish so Duncan fixed up a pole and line for him and he and Laddie spent the next hour at the stream. He did not catch anything, probably because Laddie was leaping around in the water most of the time. I'm sure most of the fish high-tailed it out of there in the first five minutes. Still, Jamie had a good time.

While we were sitting there watching Jamie, Duncan began to tell me about his plans for next summer. That was when I made a big mistake.

"Do you think your family will come up here and settle?" I asked him. I knew that many of the soldiers' families have been coming up during this past summer and I supposed his might as well.

His face got all still and he looked away from me. All the friendly and easy comradeship that had been between us was suddenly gone.

"No," he answered, and would say no more.

Shortly after that he called Jamie back and we returned to Angus's cabin.

I knew it. I knew there was something very wrong going on with him.

October 9th, 1784

I have the answer to my question and I am feeling terrible about it.

Duncan came by with a brace of ducks this afternoon. I was almost too shy to look him in the face, remembering what had happened the other day, and he seemed ill at ease as well. I did not know what to do. Then Mother sent me to the stream to fetch water and to my surprise Duncan offered to help me carry it back. We got to the stream and filled two buckets, but instead of turning back immediately, Duncan sat down on a log and motioned for me to sit beside him. What he told me next is burned into my memory. I am going to try to set down our conversation as closely as I can.

"I owe you an explanation, Mary," he said to me, his voice very low.

"No," I answered back quickly. "Of course you don't. I shouldn't have asked questions of you about your family. It was rude."

"Why in the world should you not?" he answered. "It was not rude at all. You were just being friendly." Then he got all quiet for a couple of long moments.

I did not know what to do. I found myself peeling the bark off the log, staring at it as if I'd never in my life seen a log before.

"You see, Mary . . . " he said finally, then he stopped and drew a very big breath. "You see, Mary," he repeated, "even though my mother saved Angus and me, my family are all rebels."

I must have gasped, it was so unexpected.

"Only Angus knows," he said. "I was afraid that if your family knew they would not want me around."

"They would never feel that way," I burst out. "Mother thinks of you almost as another son — I *know* that!"

"I would like to think so," he answered, but he didn't sound convinced. "But everyone here hates the rebels, and with good cause."

"Why did — ?" I began, but I bit the words back as soon as they were out of my mouth. I would not ask another personal question. Duncan must have realized what I was going to ask though, and he answered it anyway.

"My father and brothers and I had a terrible fight when this war broke out," he said, poking at the ground with a stick. "They believed firmly in the Patriots' cause, but I believed just as firmly in the Loyalists' stand."

"What happened?" The question asked itself. I could not help it.

"We went to war. My father and my two older

brothers on one side, and I on the other. And that was the last I ever saw of them. It nearly broke my mother's heart."

"What did your mother believe?"

"My mother believed in loving her family. When we were torn apart it must near have torn her apart, too."

"Do you suppose your father and brothers know she helped you escape?"

"I doubt it," he answered. "They would never forgive her."

"But you are the same family — the same blood!"

"My father disowned me when I told him I had joined the Royal Yorkers. He threw me out of the house and declared that as far as he was concerned, I was no longer a son of his."

"But that's terrible!" I could not even begin to disguise how shocked I was.

"True. But how much more terrible would it have been if I had met my father on the battlefield? Or one of my brothers? God spared me that, at least."

I could not help myself. I reached out and took hold of his hand.

"I am so sorry," I whispered.

"There's nothing to be done about it," he answered. Then he squeezed my hand tightly. "I am just fortunate that I found a place here with your family."

He stood up, drew me to my feet, and we carried the buckets of water home. Soon after, he left and I have not stopped thinking about him since.

Poor Duncan. To lose your country is bad enough, but to lose your family as well! And to know that you will never see them again. How can he bear it?

October 12th, 1784

We have harvested some small bedraggled turnip roots and a fair crop of beans. Father wants to trade with the Indians for more corn.

October 14th, 1784

Angus and Duncan shot their bear! It is enormous! Angus turned up at our doorstep early this morning and we all rushed off to see it. It has been coming around Angus's shanty for the last few nights, so finally he and Duncan laid in wait for it and when it turned up last night they shot it. They have cut it up and Mother is busy salting the meat down. We will have bear roast for dinner today and plenty of meat for the winter.

October 20th, 1784

Now that there is not so much work to do in the garden, I have been knitting and knitting and knitting. I made mittens for myself and another blanket for the new baby. Mother boiled up some dried blueberries and we soaked it in the water from them and dyed it the prettiest shade of pale blue. Then we simmered it in urine to make the colour permanent. I do not know why that works, but it does. Father says it's the acid in the urine that does it. Needless to say, when that was all finished and done with we gave the blanket a good washing!

Now I am knitting a pair of socks. Mother showed me how to turn the heel and I have already made one. It is quite neatly done if I do say so myself. Mother has knitted socks for Father and Angus, but I am knitting these for Duncan. I have not said so, though, as I do not wish to be teased.

October 25th, 1784

Pigeon pie for supper!

The pigeons are migrating and great flocks of them are flying by every day, so Father made a trap for them. He propped up a net with sticks and when they landed it fell on them. Angus came by with yet more birds that he had just knocked out of a tree. There are so many of them! Mother is making pies at a great rate and is salting down the rest. We will have pigeon pies all winter.

October 30th, 1784

The Indians came by today with a freshly killed wild turkey. They catch them in snares. We traded for some of our precious cloth and more flour. They also brought spruce and showed us how to make tea out of it. Sweetened with maple syrup, it is quite refreshing and they gave us to understand that it is healthy to drink it in the winter when we don't have fresh vegetables and berries.

Mother is busy making shirts for Father and the boys out of the buckskins that Father tanned. The Indians showed him how to do that by using the brains of the small animals he and the boys shoot. I wouldn't watch. Mother is using thread made from the fibres of basswood. The Indians showed Father how to make that, too. Mother says she will make me a buckskin skirt next. I have been admiring the buckskins the Indians wear and I cannot wait to have such a skirt.

There are two men who visit us regularly. One is older than the other and I think is the father. I wish I could talk with them. Father is slowly learning their language and has taught me a few words. I do not know their names, though, as Father has not been able to understand that much yet. Probably we will give them English names. That makes it easier for us, I suppose, but somehow doesn't seem quite right to me. They have a village not too far from here. Perhaps by next summer we will be friendly enough to visit them there. I would like to meet their wives and children. Perhaps their wives could teach me how to do the intricate beading that decorates their clothing. It is so beautiful!

November 1st, 1784

The skies are grey and gloomy and I can smell snow in the air again. Grannie says all the signs are for an early winter.

Angus has made himself a fine hat out of a raccoon skin. He has promised Jamie one and Jamie is wild with anticipation.

November 5th, 1784

Grannie and my nose were right. It is snowing. It is going to be another hard winter, I think. But how different it is from this time last year. As I write this I can look around to see Grannie spinning away and Mother sewing and humming under her breath. Father is making a cradle for the new baby and is carving the headboard into the most intricate and delicate design of roses and leaves all twisted and twining together. Jamie is whittling kindling wood. Laddie is fast asleep but his paws are jerking and he is making little whining noises. I think he is chasing rabbits in his sleep. His tail is twitching and Mittens is staring at it. I think she is about to pounce.

There was just a knock at the door and Angus and Duncan have come in, shaking snow off their caps and jackets. They have brought three rabbits that they snared. They are going to stay the night.

Later

I managed to give Duncan his socks this evening after everyone else had gone to bed. I peeked down from the loft and saw him sitting by the fire, staring into it. I have not been able to stop thinking about what he told me. He must be so lonely here, knowing he will never see his family again.

Angus was stretched out on a blanket in the corner, Grannie was sound asleep in her bed, and all was quiet behind Mother and Father's curtain. I had not changed into my nightdress yet, so I gathered up my courage and crept down the ladder.

"Here," I whispered, and thrust the socks at

Duncan. I would have turned and scampered back up immediately, but he caught me by the arm before I could do so.

"Are these for me?" he asked. "Did you knit them?"

"Yes," I managed to say. It is fortunate that the light was so dim as I knew my face was flaming with embarrassment.

"Thank you," he said. "I've never had a better present." Then he smiled and this time his eyes smiled too. I fairly flew back up the ladder.

I can hardly see to write, the wick I have been using is guttering and I must blow it out. I have come to the end of the pages in this journal, but my birthday is next month and I will ask Father if he could find a new one for me. This writing in a journal is a habit I find I cannot break. Nor do I want to.

The wind is howling outside, but all is safe and peaceful in this little house. We still do not have much. We will have to husband our supplies very carefully to get through this winter, but I am certain we will make it.

And tomorrow I will start on a quilt.

Epilogue

That first winter was difficult; some of the Loyalists did not survive. Mary and her family did, however, as did the Ross family. In the spring of 1785 Mary's new "Canadian" sister, Ann, was born. She was a healthy, happy baby.

The Loyalists cleared more land, planted crops, and brought in a good harvest at the season's end.

Angus and Molly were married — Hannah and Mary were delighted to become sisters. Mr. MacDonald started up the school in the spring and they were amongst his most enthusiastic pupils.

Mary and Duncan were married in the summer of 1787. Unfortunately, that was just before the time that came to be known as "The Hungry Year." The Government supplies were discontinued, the belief being that the Loyalists would be settled enough by then to support themselves, but there was a drought and all the grain crops failed that summer. The winter that followed was one of starvation, and many settlers died, including, to Mary's great sorrow, her beloved Grannie. Mary gave birth to a child in the spring of 1788, but the boy was stillborn. It was a terrible year for her and for the whole family.

Mary gave birth to a girl the next year, however, when conditions had improved, and this child flourished. She was named Margaret. Mary went on to have five more children, two more girls and three boys.

By the time Upper Canada was declared to be a separate province, the MacDonald family was well established. They had not seen the last of war, however. Duncan and their three sons were called upon to join the Canadian Militia and fight in the War of 1812 when the Americans invaded Canada. They survived the fighting, to Mary's everlasting gratitude, but one son, Robert, was badly wounded.

Hannah Ross and Alex Calder were married the year after Mary and Duncan, and Hannah gave birth to a boy not two months after Mary's daughter was born. They had four more children, one of whom did die in the Battle of Crysler's Farm in 1813.

Mr. MacDonald gave up teaching in his sixtieth year. He died soon after; Mary's mother the following year.

Jamie became the owner of a prosperous country store. He was never without a dog. Cats abounded, many of them descendants of Mittens herself. Mary's younger sister, Ann, never married. She lived with Mary and Duncan and was a beloved aunt to their children. She it was who inherited their Grannie's healing ways, and her herbs and simples kept the family hale and healthy.

Mary died in her eightieth year, two years after Duncan, surrounded by her children, grandchildren, and several great-grandchildren. She was one of the oldest and most respected citizens of Johnstown.

The lilac bush Grannie planted in their doorway grew, and thrived, and blossomed every spring.

Historical Note

By 1775 Britain's thirteen colonies in America were becoming more and more dissatisfied with their mother country. Among other complaints, they believed that Britain and the British Parliament were interfering too much in their affairs. Most particularly, they felt that the colonies were being subjected to unfair taxes when they had no vote or representation of their own in Britain. Finally, this dissatisfaction increased to such an extent that some men and women believed the only solution was to take up arms, dissolve their ties with Britain and establish a new, independent nation in North America. These men and women, who called themselves Patriots, declared war on Britain.

Other men and women living in the colonies, equally committed, fought on the side of the British to preserve the unity of the British Empire in America. These people came to be called Loyalists because of their loyalty to Britain and King George III. These divided loyalties within the colonies led to a bloody civil war. Brothers fought against brothers, fathers against sons. Neighbours who had lived in peace and harmony together for generations turned against each other.

The war lasted for eight long years until the Patriots finally achieved victory in 1783 and a new country, the United States of America, was born. The preliminary treaty of peace between Britain and the United States of America was signed on November 30, 1782. The final version, joined to peace treaties with France and Spain, would not be signed until September, 1783. However, the terms of the agreement were made known in New York City in March, and the formal cessation of hostilities took place on April 19, 1783. Britain made a total and unconditional recognition of the independence and sovereignty of the United States of America.

After the war ended, the Loyalists who had sided with the English were driven out of the new United States of America. Their homes and farms were destroyed or stolen, many men were tarred and feathered, run out of their own towns, or even hanged. Some of these Loyalists returned to Britain, some settled in the British West Indies. As recompense for their loyalty, Britain offered free grants of land to all those who wished to go to Canada, as well as enough supplies to sustain them until such time as they could manage to support themselves. Many Loyalists accepted this offer and settled in the British North American Provinces of Nova Scotia (which at that time included New Brunswick), Prince Edward Island (then called the Island of St. John), Québec (Lower Canada), and that part of Québec which later was called Upper Canada and finally became Ontario. These settlers were farmers, frontiersmen and city dwellers, Native peoples, Black slaves and freedmen. They included those who had immigrated to America from Germany, Holland and the British Isles, including Scotland. Many were members of religious and cultural minorities. They were joined by members of the British nobility who had served as officers, and other soldiers who had fought during the war in the British Army or the Loyalist regiments. (These Loyalist regiments were called the Provincial Corps because of their affiliation with particular provinces in the thirteen colonies of America.) In all, the thirteen former American colonies lost almost 80,000 valuable citizens.

The royal province of New York remained a British and Loyalist stronghold throughout the war, and numerous Loyalist corps were affiliated with this colony. As the war drew to a close and it became apparent that the Patriots would win, New York City became a gathering place for many of these and other refugees until November of 1783.

Some Loyalist settlers made their way north by

land to the forts established in such places as Sorel, Lachine and Machiche along the shores of the St. Lawrence River in Québec. There, families were reunited with husbands, fathers and brothers who had served in the armies. Shelters were built for them, schools were started. The Loyalists wintered over in these makeshift settlements. Then, the following spring, they spread out to the permanent settlements along the St. Lawrence that Sir Frederick Haldimand, Governor of Québec, had acquired for them.

The Iroquois, a federation of Six Nations whose lands straddled the Mohawk Valley, had for the most part sided with the British. At the close of the war they found that the British had broken their promises to them and had ceded all of their lands to the Americans. The Iroquois, too, became displaced persons and were forced to emigrate north to Canada. To compensate them, they were also given land in Canada and, under the leadership of their Chief, Joseph Brant, many settled in the Niagara region. Others took refuge under the leadership of Chiefs John Deseronto, Isaac Hill and Aaron Hill and were settled in the Bay of Quinte region along the north shore of Lake Ontario.

While many of the Loyalists were treated well by the British government, the same cannot be said of the Blacks who were loyal to the British and who even fought on the British side.

In 1775 Sir John Murray, Earl of Dunmore and Royal Governor of Virginia, issued a proclamation promising freedom to any escaped slave who would join the British forces. When the war was over they too were promised land and supplies enough to start a new life. As well, Brigadier General Samuel Birch, the British army chief, issued a permit which came to be called a "General Birch Certificate" to any Black man who could prove that he had been behind the British lines for twelve months and was not a British slave. Many of these people took ship from New York to Nova Scotia. However, the promises made to them were not kept. They found themselves living in abject poverty, and a great number of them fled to Sierra Leone in Africa where, unfortunately, circumstances were not much better.

Slaves belonging to Loyalists were not freed, although their Loyalist masters began referring to them not as slaves but as "servants." Many Loyaists brought their slaves with them to Canada. The trade in slavery had been abolished in Britain in 1774, but it was not until 1793 that John Graves Simcoe secured the consent of the Upper Canadian Assembly to an act which made buying and selling slaves illegal in Canada, and declared that children of slaves would be free on reaching their twenty-fifth birthday.

During the winter of 1783 members of Sir John Johnson's 2nd Battalion started construction around Fort Niagara. They built houses, the first two of which were for Joseph Brant and his sister Molly. Dwellings, grist mills and sawmills were also begun at Cataraqui in order to be ready for the settlers who had taken refuge in Québec along the St. Lawrence River.

At first there was a great resistance amongst these Loyalists to move so much farther west along the St. Lawrence. Many of them still believed that they would be able to return to their homes in the new United States and resume their former lives. They were worried about the distance they would have to travel, and had heard about the fearsome rapids that impeded navigation up the St. Lawrence. They also knew that they would need much assistance from Governor Haldimand if they were to survive. Most of them had lost almost everything they owned. They had no cattle, no horses or oxen, or the necessary farming tools. Nor did they have money to purchase them. They knew they would not be able to develop new lands or even to feed themselves during the initial work of building and clearing, and that they would not be able to succeed without a steady supply of equipment and provisions over several years. Governor Haldimand recognized their needs and promised to address them. In March of 1784 authorization arrived from Britain that the Loyalists would receive the aid they required. Thus reassured, the number of volunteers for Upper Canada increased.

Regimental loyalties provided the only communities most of the Loyalists still had. The knowledge that they would settle in Upper Canada with the regiments of their own fathers and brothers helped to commit many of the undecided to the new territories.

Governor Haldimand had entered into a series of negotiations with the Mississauga chiefs and councils, and during 1783 they provided Haldimand's government with all the property it would need for 10,000 Loyalists and Iroquois. Late in 1783 surveyor John Collins began marking out the new townships. At that time Governor Haldimand advised the Iroquois and the Loyalists to prepare for the migration to their new homes in the spring of 1784.

In May, 1784, as soon as the river was free of ice, the Loyalists began to gather at the town of Lachine, at the foot of the rapids just west of Montréal. At Lachine Captain Jacob Maurer had been busy all winter, chartering river boats called *bateaux* (normally used by fur-traders) requisitioning tents and cloth, ordering thousands of hoes and axes from the military smiths, and stockpiling provisions and seed. With these preparations, the westward movement proceeded quickly. Despite the inevitable confusion and crowding, Captain Maurer was able to begin sending the Loyalists upriver before the end of May. Flotillas of a dozen *bateaux* began departing, with each boat carrying four or five families, a ton or two of provisions and household effects, and a crew of five experienced boatmen. By the end of June, the last of the Loyalists had departed, eventually reaching new settlements which stretched all the way from Johnstown (now Cornwall) to Cataraqui, and eventually on into the Niagara region.

When the first Loyalists landed at the different points along the shores, most of the lots had not yet been marked out by the surveyors. The settlers were obliged to wait several weeks before the drawings of lots could take place. They had brought with them a number of military tents, which had seen service during the Revolutionary War, but every day lost meant one day less for them to prepare for the coming winter. This caused great concern. The settlers had no alternative, however, but to pitch their tents near where they had landed and wait until the surveyors had completed their work, which was not until near the end of summer — too late for planting most crops.

When the drawings for lots took place, small pieces of paper with the appropriate lot numbers were placed in a hat and the surveyor, with a map spread out before him, oversaw the whole business. The officers drew first for lots in the first concession, fronting upon the water. After the officers, the other members of the community drew for their lots. Civilians received 50 acres if single, 100 if the head of a family, and 50 acres for each member of the family. Privates got the same allotment, while non-commissioned officers received 200 acres, and so on up the scale to field officers — colonel and above — who got 1000 acres.

The Loyalists began clearing the forests and building homes for themselves as soon as their lots had been apportioned. The work was harsh, made even more difficult by the shortage of horses and oxen. Cows were in short supply, as were other farm animals. There was plentiful game to be had, however, and the river teemed with fish. The Native peoples who lived there, the Mississauga, helped the newcomers in many ways. They taught them much about finding the edible roots and medicinal herbs that grew wild around them, also much about methods of grinding corn without the kinds of mills the settlers were used to, and how to fish for the sturgeon, whitefish, salmon and many other species that filled the rivers.

Governor Haldimand supplied the Loyalists with clothes, food, axes, hoes, spades and seed, and provided a few sawmills and grist mills. The first winter was hard, but most of the Loyalists survived. In the spring of 1785 they were quick to plant their crops, and that year could harvest their corn, potatoes, turnips and other vegetables.

The Government ceased sending supplies to the settlers in 1787 on the supposition that by this time they would be self-sufficient. They would have been, but that summer a severe drought caused the grain crops to fail. This, combined with a lack of supplies and a very harsh winter, resulted in a widespread famine. The following year came to be known as "The Hungry Year," when many of the settlers starved to death. They were reduced to eating the buds of the basswood tree, and stories are told of a single beef bone being passed from family to family to be boiled and reboiled.

By 1790 more and more land was cleared and crops increased. More sawmills and grist mills appeared, even the occasional country store, stocked with goods from Montréal. More emigrants had come from across the border, and because of a high birth rate the settlers' numbers were increasing quickly. New townships opened up, schools were started. Finally, Upper Canada was declared a separate province in 1791, covering very much the area now occupied by southern Ontario.

His Majeſty's PROVINCIAL REGIMENT, *called* The King's Royal Regiment of New York whereof Sir John Johnson Knight & Baronet is Lieut Colonel Commandant.

THESE are to Certify, that the Bearer hereof Duncan McKenzie ——— in Capt. Rd. Duncan's Company, of the aforeſaid Regiment, born in the Pariſh of Artola ——— in the County of Invernefs —Aged Twenty one Years Hath ſerved honeſtly and faithfully in the ſaid Regiment Four — Years; and in conſequence of His Majeſty's Order for Diſbanding the ſaid Regiment, he is hereby Diſcharged, and is intitled, by His Majeſty's late Order, to the Portion of Land allotted to each Soldier of His Provincial Corps who wiſhes to become a Settler in this Province. He having firſt received all juſt demands of Pay, Cloathing, &c. from his entry into the ſaid Regiment, to the Date of his Diſcharge, as appears by his Receipt on the Back hereof.

GIVEN under my Hand and Seal at Arms — — at Montreal — — — this Twenty fourth Day of December — 1783

John Johnson

Discharge papers such as this were given to men when their regiments disbanded.

Not drooping like poor fugitives they came
In exodus to our Canadian wilds,
But full of heart and hope, with heads erect
And fearless eyes, victorious in defeat.

— *William Kirby*

Loyalists in an oxen-drawn team ready to board a raft and cross a river on their way to Canada.

Mohawk leader Joseph Brant, also known as Thayendanegea, led his people northwest to the Niagara region after their lands had been ceded to the Patriots following the war of independence.

A depiction of the Loyalists' encampment at Johnstown, later called Cornwall, on June 6, 1784.

A southeast view of Cataraqui, which was later named Kingston.

To His Excellency Lieutenant General Haldimand Governor & Commander in Chief, &c., &c.

"The request of the Companies of Associated Loyalists going to form a Settlement at Cataraque.

"That Boards, Nails and Shingls be found each Family for Compleating such Buildings as they shall see Cause to Erect for their Convenience at any time for the space of Two years from & after their first Arrival at Cataraque with Eighty Squares of Window Glass to be delivered shortly after their arrival there.

"That Arms & Ammunition with one Felling Ax be allowed for each Male Inhabitant of the age of fourteen years

"Be allowed for each family:

One Plough shear & Coulter
Leather for Horse Collers
Two Spades
Three Iron Wedges
Fifteen Iron Harrow Teeth
Three Hoes
One Inch & half Inch Auger
Three Chisels (sorted)
One Gouge
Three Gimblets
One Hand Saw & Files
One Nail Hammer
One Drawing Knife
One Frow for splitting Shingles
Two Scythes & one Sickle
One Broad Ax

One Grind stone allowed for every Three families.

One years Clothing to be issued to Each Family in proportion to their Numbers in the different species of Articles Issued to those gone to Nova Scotia.

Two years Provisions to be found to Each Family in Proportion to their Number and Age.

Two Horses, Two Cows and six Sheep to be delivered at Cataroque to Each Family at Government's Expence. The Cost of which to be made known at delivery To the End that the same may by a Moderate Tax, be again repaid to Government at the End of Ten years if required — Our present Poverty & Inability to Purchase these Articles as well as our remote situation when there from Wealthy Inhabitants, will we hope pleed our Excuse in this respect.

"That seeds of different kinds such as Wheat, Indian Corn, Pease, Oats, Potatoes & Flax seed be given to each Family in quantity as His Excellency may think proper.

"That one Blacksmith be Established in each Township & found with Tools & Iron for Two years at Government Expence for the use of the Inhabitants of each Town.

"SOREL the ____ January 1784"

Text of a 1784 petition from Loyalists to General Haldimand, requesting supplies.

Loyalists draw lots for land in 1784.

Dense forests made clearing the land in western Québec (later known as Upper Canada, and eventually Ontario) a massive job.

It took so long to get rid of stumps that at first the crops were planted between them.

Pounding grain and making soap, chinking log walls and chopping wood, were some of the many chores in store for the Loyalist settlers.

Recipes

Johnnycake

Take 2 cups buttermilk, add 2 cups cornmeal, pinch salt, 2 spoonfuls molasses, sugar or maple syrup and 2 well-beaten eggs if available.
Pour batter into pan to bake.

Sops

Pour warm milk over bread and add sugar or maple syrup.

Lumpy Dick

Add flour to boiling water slowly until it turns into mush. Add a pinch of salt and serve with milk and sugar.

Bread

To warm water in which potatoes have boiled, add half a cup of sugar and 1 starter of yeast. Let this stand overnight. Then mix in half a panful of flour, 1 spoonful of salt, and a knob of lard.
Knead well. Let rise, then form into loaves.

Preserving Fish for the Winter

Boil and mash a quantity of potatoes. Spoon a layer of mashed potatoes into the bottom of a barrel. Sprinkle with salt.
Boil fish until it flakes easily.
Hold fish by the tail over the layer of potatoes in the barrel and shake until all the flesh falls off.
Spoon another layer of potatoes and salt over the fish.
Shake more fish over the potatoes.
Continue layering fish and potatoes alternately until the barrel is full.
Place barrel outside the kitchen door where it will freeze.
Dig out or slice off as much as is needed at a time and fry into fishcakes.

Quilting bees were as much social events as a time to help a neighbour — who often lived miles away — finish a quilt.

Old and young alike helped in the gathering of sap and boiling it down to make maple syrup.

One of the earliest Loyalist settlements in Upper Canada.

Two men spearing salmon from a canoe in Lower Canada.

Only after many tree stumps were cleared — a huge job — could the settlers sow grain.

Loyalist settlers camping alongside a river on their journey to British North America.

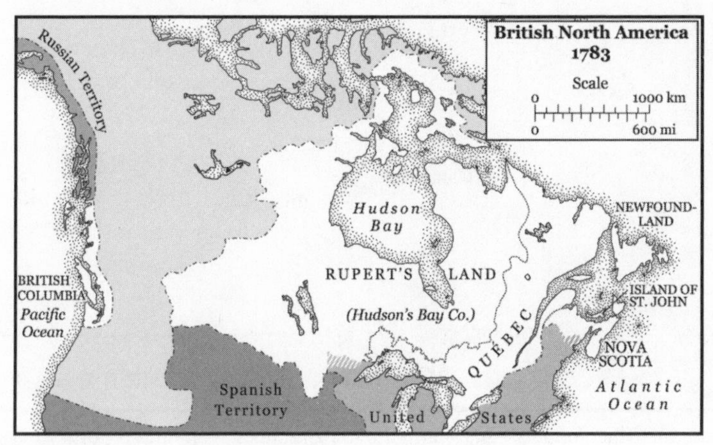

British North America in 1783.

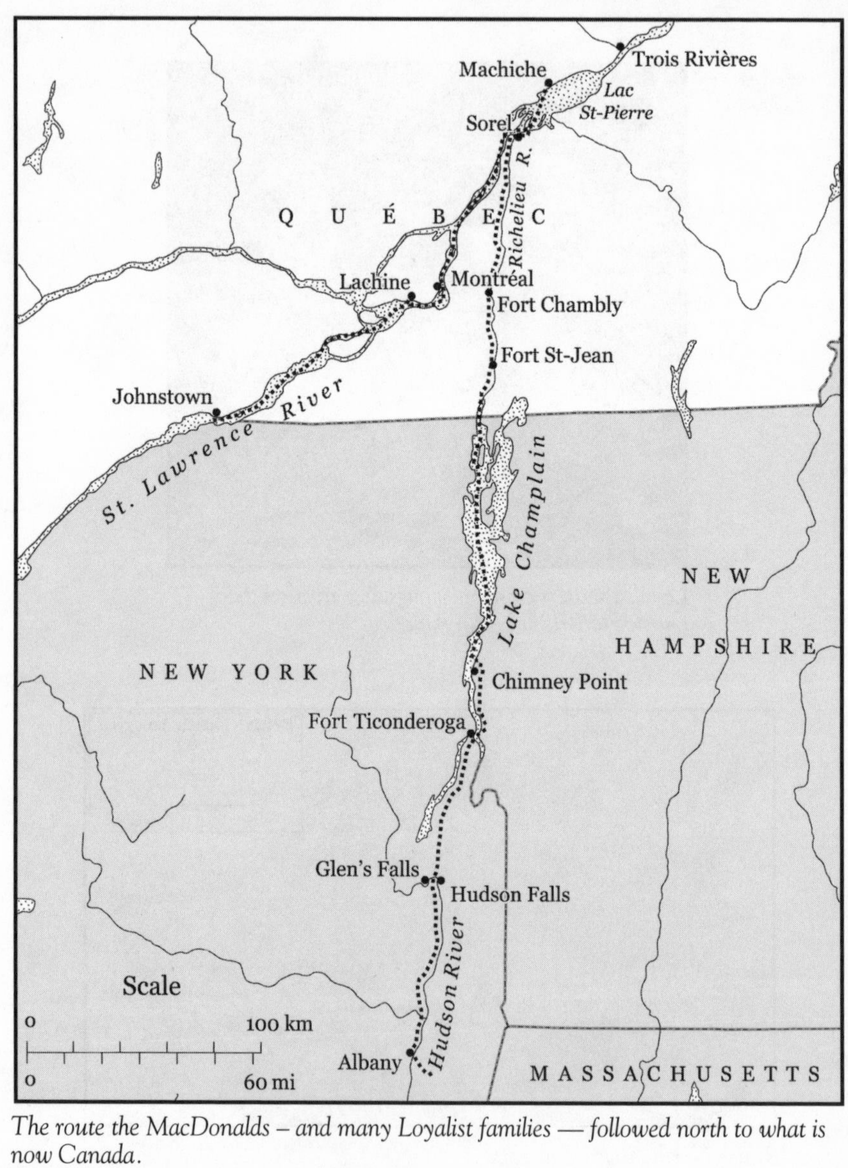

The route the MacDonalds – and many Loyalist families — followed north to what is now Canada.

Acknowledgments

Grateful acknowledgment is made for permission to reprint the following:

Cover portrait: National Gallery of Scotland, Robert Herdman, *Evening Thoughts,* detail (NG 2136).

Cover background: The Loyalist Flag, photograph by Andrea Casault.

Page 205 (upper): William Kirby, 1817-1906.

Page 205 (lower): National Archives of Canada, Charles William Jefferys, C20587.

Page 206: National Gallery of Canada, Ottawa. *Thayendanegea (Joseph Brant),* c. 1807 by William Berczy, purchased 1951, #5777.

Page 207 (upper): National Archives of Canada, James Peachey, *Encampment of the Loyalists at Johnstown (Cornwall) June 6, 1784,* C2001.

Page 207 (lower): National Archives of Canada, James Peachey, *A South-East View of Cataraqui (Kingston),* C1511.

Page 208: From E. A. Cruikshank, ed., *The Settlement of the United Empire Loyalists, Toronto,* Ontario Historical Society, 1934, pp. 41-42.

Pages 209, 210 and 212: National Archives of Canada. J.E. Laughlin, *U.S. Loyalists Drawing Lots for Land 1784,* C13993; *Clearing the Land Around the First Cabin,* C5466; *Hoeing in the Seed,* C13995; *Pounding Grain and Making Soap,* C13997; *A Quilting Bee,* C13999; *Making Maple Sugar and Syrup,* C14000.

Page 213 (upper): National Archives of Canada, Edward Scrope Shrapnel, *One of the Earliest Loyalist Settlements in Upper Canada,* C23633.

Page 213 (lower): National Archives of Canada, Susan Haliburton Weldon, *Salmon Spearing in Lower Canada,* C121921.

Page 214: Government of Ontario Art Collection, Charles W. Jefferys, *The Pioneer, 1784,* c. 1926, watercolour on paper, 623327.
Page 215 (upper): National Archives of Canada, Charles W. Jefferys, *Loyalists Camping on the Way up the St. Lawrence,* C73449.
Pages 215 (lower) and 216: Maps by Paul Heersink/ Paperglyphs. Map data © 2000 Government of Canada with permission from Natural Resources Canada.

Thanks to Barbara Hehner for her careful checking of the manuscript, and Dr. Jane Errington for sharing her historical expertise.

For my husband, Jim,
with many thanks for all his support.

I would like to thank
Gavin K. Watt, B.A. Sc., C.M.H., Editor,
The King's Royal Regiment of New York;
Robert Stacey, Arts Associates, Toronto, Ontario;
and the staff at the National Archives
in Ottawa, Ontario.

About the Author

Many of Karleen Bradford's books are inspired by places she has visited. She was born in Toronto, but moved to Argentina when she was nine. After coming back to Canada to attend the University of Toronto, she married a foreign service officer with the Canadian Government . . . and began thirty-four years of additional travelling, from Colombia and England to the Philippines and Germany. It was in Germany that Karleen began tracing the route of the Crusaders, and became so intrigued with that period of history that she wrote *There Will Be Wolves*, winner of the CLA Best Young Adult Novel Award. The Crusades story continues with *Shadows on a Sword* and *Lionheart's Scribe.* To research the stories, Karleen and her husband actually retraced the Crusaders' footsteps from Cologne, in Germany, to Istanbul, Turkey.

Karleen has written sixteen books for young readers. Some are historical (*The Nine Days Queen*). But she writes in many other genres as well: fantasy (*The Other Elizabeth*), contemporary fiction (*Another Kind of Champion*) and non-fiction (*Write Now!* and *Animal Heroes*). Her many awards include the CLA Best Young Adult Novel, an ALA

Best Book citation, and nominations for the Silver Birch Award, the Geoffrey Bilson Historical Award and the Manitoba Reader's Choice Award.

True to her usual research routine, Karleen travelled through New York State, along Lake Champlain and up into Québec, along the route Mary MacDonald and her family would have taken, when she was writing *With Nothing But Our Courage.* It is this kind of attention to the smells and appearance and feel of a place or setting that helps Karleen's books feel so very real to the reader.

What is about writing that has Karleen so hooked on it? "As far back as I can remember," she says, "my favourite activity was curling up in a corner somewhere with a book." She was such an avid writer, even as a child, that she would create plays for her friends to act in, even when they weren't as eager as *she* was. She once heard a group of friends say, "Oh, no! Karleen's written another play and she's going to make us act in it." And she did.

No matter that Karleen has actually *lived* in more countries than most people visit, there always remains one constant in her life — another writing project on the go.

National Library of Canada Cataloguing in Publication Data

Bradford, Karleen
With nothing but our courage :
the Loyalist diary of Mary MacDonald

(Dear Canada)
ISBN 0-439-98979-5

1. United Empire Loyalists – Juvenile fiction.
I. Title. II. Series.

PS8553.R217W58 2002 jC813'.54 C2001-903372-9

6 5 4 Printed in Canada 03 04 05

The display type was set in Ellington.
The text was set in Cochin.

Printed in Canada
First printing, January 2002

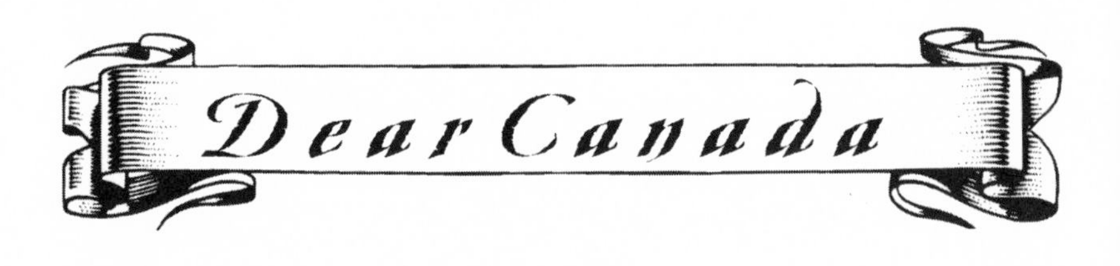

A Prairie as Wide as the Sea
The Immigrant Diary of Ivy Weatherall
by Sarah Ellis

Orphan at My Door
The Home Child Diary of Victoria Cope
by Jean Little

Footsteps in the Snow
The Red River Diary of Isobel Scott
by Carol Matas

A Ribbon of Shining Steel
The Railway Diary of Kate Cameron
by Julie Lawson

Whispers of War
The War of 1812 Diary of Susanna Merritt
by Kit Pearson

Alone in an Untamed Land
The Filles du Roi *Diary of Hélène St. Onge*
by Maxine Trottier

Brothers Far from Home
The World War I Diary of Eliza Bates
by Jean Little